Whoever the man was, he seemed to have stopped trailing her.

At two in the morning, her thoughts on sleep, Carly retrieved her keys from her handbag. Then she heard the footsteps behind her. A warning sensation skittered through her, but she made herself look back.

He stood a few feet away, beneath a street lamp. "Can we talk?"

Whatever the man had to say didn't matter. Carly couldn't afford to get mugged and end up in a hospital. Who would take care of Billy? She was all he had. She quickened her stride and bolted up her steps. Only then did she whirl around. "What do you want?" she demanded.

"My son." He spoke so softly she barely heard him.

"What?"

With a subtle shift of his body, he seemed to move closer. "You have my son."

Dear Reader,

Book #1000?! In February, 1982, when Silhouette Special Edition was first published, that seemed a far distant goal. And now, almost fourteen years later, here we are!

We're opening CELEBRATION 1000 with a terrific book from the beloved Diana Palmer—*Maggie's Dad*. Diana was one of the first authors to contribute to Special Edition, and now she's returned with this tender tale of love reborn.

Lindsay McKenna continues her action-packed new series, MORGAN'S MERCENARIES: LOVE AND DANGER. The party goes on with *Logan's Bride* by Christine Flynn— the first HOLIDAY ELOPEMENTS, three tales of love and weddings over the holiday season. And join the festivities with wonderful stories by Jennifer Mikels, Celeste Hamilton and Brittany Young.

We have so many people to thank for helping us to reach this milestone. Silhouette Special Edition would not be what it is today without our marvelous writers. I want to take a moment, though, to mention one author—Sondra Stanford. She gave us Book #7, *Silver Mist*, and many other wonderful stories. We lost her in October 1991 after a valiant struggle against cancer. We miss her; she brought a great deal of happiness to all who knew her.

And our very special thanks to our readers. Your imaginations and brave hearts allow books to take flight— and all of us can never thank you enough for that!

The celebration continues in December and January—with books by Nora Roberts, Debbie Macomber, Sherryl Woods and many more of your favorite writers! Happy Book 1000—to each and every romantic!

Sincerely,

Tara Gavin, Senior Editor

Please address questions and book requests to:
Silhouette Reader Service
U.S.: 3010 Walden Ave., P.O. Box 1325, Buffalo, NY 14269
Canadian: P.O. Box 609, Fort Erie, Ont. L2A 5X3

JENNIFER MIKELS

CHILD OF MINE

Silhouette®

SPECIAL EDITION®

Published by Silhouette Books

America's Publisher of Contemporary Romance

For Dan, with love.

For Karen Taylor Richman, my editor,
And for Laurie Feigenbaum, my agent,
a sincere thanks to both of you.

 SILHOUETTE BOOKS

ISBN 0-373-09993-2

CHILD OF MINE

Copyright © 1995 by Suzanne Kuhlin

Books by Jennifer Mikels

Silhouette Special Edition

A Sporting Affair #66
Whirlwind #124
Remember the Daffodils #478
Double Identity #521
Stargazer #574
Freedom's Just Another Word #623
A Real Charmer #694
A Job for Jack #735
Your Child, My Child #807
Denver's Lady #870
Jake Ryker's Back in Town #929
Sara's Father #947
Child of Mine #993

Silhouette Romance

Lady of the West #462
Maverick #487
Perfect Partners #511
The Bewitching Hour #551

JENNIFER MIKELS

started out an avid fan of historical novels, which eventually led her to contemporary romances, which in turn led her to try her hand at penning her own novels. She quickly found she preferred romance fiction with its happy endings to the technical writing she'd done for a public relations firm. Between writing and raising two boys, the Phoenix-based author has little time left for hobbies, though she does enjoy cross-country skiing and antique shopping with her husband.

Dear Reader,

Writing contemporary love stories is a dream come true for me, one that started ten years ago with a typewriter on the kitchen table and two noisy boys repeatedly racing through the room and slamming doors. Life has changed around me since then. The typewriter has been replaced by a computer, and those boys have become young men. But my pleasure in creating many different characters and relating how they fall in love has never faded.

What I enjoy most is delving into the world of today's single woman who is forced to wear so many hats while she juggles career, home and, sometimes, motherhood. I love finding a perfect man for her, one who understands the demands on her, who arouses passion and offers hope and who makes her a believer again in—what we all want—love.

This kind of man is the ultimate hero. He brings real romance to a woman through friendship and laughter. He reveals a capacity to love not only her but, in some instances, also her child.

Next year, Silhouette Special Edition will publish two more of my books. One of them is about Mara Vincetti, a young mother with a newborn, who finds one of these ultimate heroes.

I'm pleased to be a part of the celebration honoring Silhouette Special Edition's 1000th book and to be able to tell love stories that are realistic, mature and emotional.

Jennifer Mikels

Chapter One

"This is the third night he's been here."

Carly Mitchell shot a look over her shoulder at the customer Renee Thompson was ogling. With his hand cupped around a glass of bourbon and water, he sat at a small round table in Dawn's station. For that, Carly thanked the angel who kept a watchful eye over cocktail waitresses. The base of her neck had tingled from his continuous stare ever since his arrival half an hour ago. Carly had met the man's cool green eyes, only briefly, because they trapped with their directness.

"Is he *something?*"

Something, Carly agreed. He had the air of a man used to wielding power. In his mid-thirties, he had a smooth, lightly tanned complexion, and unlike some of the other executive types who came in here, a lean body that indicated diligent efforts at racquetball or swimming or some health club torture. Instead of being conservatively cut, his dark hair hung a touch too long in back, brushing the collar of his shirt. Carly noted the distinct slash of cheekbones, the sensual mouth, the strength of his jaw. She felt a pull that set off a warning within her. This stirring for a stranger surprised her, but she savored the sensation because it had been so long since she'd felt it.

Beneath the dim lights, he'd given the impression of a man born with a silver spoon in his mouth. Ivy League graduate. Intelligent. An expert in the New York stock exchange whose favorite reading material included *The Wall Street Journal* and financial magazines.

His perfectly tailored dark suit, one her uncle would have nodded approvingly at, identified him as a typical customer of Top Hat, the hotel's lounge. Many of them wandered into the place after indulging in pheasant under glass or rack of lamb.

Typical customers ranged from executives on business trips to bored yuppies clamoring to fit in with Denver's elite. They all shared a common goal—an eagerness for fun. All of them except him. He appeared dead set against even smiling.

A stuffed shirt, Carly mused, and definitely the wrong type for her. But because it was her nature, she started to smile, offering a token of friendliness. She was a people person, the kind who would say hello to someone passing her on the street.

This time her smile froze before it could form as she noticed his gaze traveling up her. She'd been the recipient of lecherous looks that had bothered her less. There was nothing lascivious or seductive in his once-over. Annoyed, she met his critical stare squarely, even as she sensed he was used to intimidating with it. *Not this time, buster. You've met your match.* She waited a second longer than necessary just to prove she wasn't unnerved, then presented her back to him, but her stomach somersaulted in mockery of her cool manner.

"Looks like money," Renee murmured, reaching behind Carly for cocktail napkins and a stirrer located at a far corner of the bar.

Carly spoke her thought aloud. "Not too friendly-looking." Her eyes shifted to Renee's costume. High at the neck and sleeveless, the tuxedo top clung but showed no hint of flesh. The bottom of the costume bared legs and enticed the eye but revealed no more than a bathing suit would. Carly straightened her friend's bow tie. With a teenage sister to support, she needed her job as much as Carly did.

Tipping her head, Renee's reddish curls shone beneath the subdued lighting. "Am I perfect?"

Carly laughed. "Perfect."

"Then I'd better get a move on." She mumbled something about table five and an oilman from Texas.

Carly had one of them, too.

Behind her, the bartender slid a tall glass and two bottles in her direction. "Here's your margarita, Carly."

"Thanks, Vince." She placed the cocktail and two beers on her tray and left the bar to deliver her orders.

Dressed in a Western-style suit and a Stetson, the Texan's hand brushed hers as she placed his drink before him. "Thank ya, ma'am."

Carly swept up the bills he'd placed at the edge of the table and returned a smile meant to be pleasant but not encouraging, then skimmed by the patrons at her other tables. A couple in the corner, draped all over each other, hadn't touched their drinks.

"I need a vodka tonic, Vince," Carly called out a step from the bar.

Sidling close to her, Renee nudged her with an elbow. "Wish me luck. I traded tables with Dawn."

Carly gave her a good-luck smile. Better thee than me. She liked men with a sense of humor, men who smiled and laughed a lot, easygoing men who knew how to have fun. The object of Renee's attention looked like one of those business types who would sprinkle crumbs of affection out to the woman in his life if he had time between financial coups.

"Wouldn't you know it?" Renee pulled a face. "He's leaving. And look who took his place."

Discreetly, Carly glanced back then laughed as an Alfred Hitchcock look-alike settled on the vacated chair.

"Very funny," Renee mumbled.

For the first time in the past forty minutes, Carly no longer felt like tugging at the back of the high-cut legs of her costume. Usually she skirted around tables and never gave the costume's brevity a second thought. After months of working at Top Hat, she'd become immune to the stares at her legs. She considered them one of her finest assets. But tonight had been different, and she knew why. One man had unnerved her.

She gave her head a shake to forget about him. She had another male to think about. After she delivered an order for a bourbon and a scotch and water, she wound her way around tables toward the public telephone in the back of the lounge.

She plunked coins in the slot and punched out Miriam Bonwick's number.

"Hi, Carly," her neighbor said as a greeting because it was exactly eight-thirty and Carly's time to call.

"Is he near?" Carly asked.

"Right here."

"Hi, Billy. How's my boy?" Carly laughed as her nephew babbled back at her in the predictable fashion of a seven-month-old. Was it her imagination or had he managed a childish version of her name? "Yes, it's Carly," she answered, wanting to believe Billy knew her name. "You go to bed now. Sweet dreams."

"He just finished his bottle," Miriam informed her.

A little ache nudged at Carly's heart. Though she fed her nephew his breakfast and lunch, she never was home for the dinner hour. "How did he like the peas?"

"I'm wearing them."

Carly laughed again. "He definitely has a mind of his own." Peripherally, Carly caught the manager's scowl. "I'd better go. I'll pick him up at the usual time, Miriam."

Drumming up her brightest smile, Carly passed Roland Caldwell and sidestepped another waitress burdened with a full tray, then greeted some newly arrived customers, the first of many who would stroll in before closing.

At two in the morning, the city streets were deserted. The neighborhood was declining, buildings getting older, gangs getting stronger. Still, Carly hummed to herself and walked unconcerned. She was comfortable walking the streets at night. She often talked to strangers. Though not reckless, she simply believed that a person couldn't live, really live, if they were paranoid about everything.

On the final block before her apartment, she drew in a deep breath. The lingering aroma of garlic from a neighbor's dinner drifted to her on the cool summer breeze. She never understood why people allowed themselves to miss so much. The smells, sounds, sights of the city beckoned for a person's attention. She tried to capture it all to memory. An impossible task. But still she tried.

Dressed in jeans and a baggy sweatshirt, she stared down at her sneakers. Dirty and worn, they needed to be replaced, but she would make do with them. Her next paycheck was slated to pay a pediatrician's bill.

At the sound of footsteps behind her, a rarity during her walk home, she looked over her shoulder. Instantly, her cheerful mood slithered away.

He was behind her. The man she'd seen earlier at Top Hat. Though the darkness of night mantled his eyes, she knew they were green.

She'd never been the type to scream while watching scary movies. She wasn't skittish by nature, but the inevitable anxiousness when a woman walking alone at night realized she was being followed slammed into her.

Quickly she fished inside her oversize shoulder bag for the pepper spray attached to her key chain. Not once during the four months she'd been walking home after midnight from the lounge had she used it.

She let her mind clear for a second and tried to ignore the quickening beat of her heart. Being followed annoyed as well as frightened her. Courage in place, she pivoted around to give him a few choice words.

He was gone.

While she wanted to believe she'd scared him off, that seemed unlikely. At five foot six, she was no match for a six-footer. Laughing at herself, she dashed up the steps to her apartment. He hadn't been following her, she decided. More likely, he'd simply been in the same place at the same time.

Alex Kane was annoyed. For days, he'd been trying to determine how to approach her. He prided himself on being able to key in on people. That was what had made him successful. But Carly Mitchell puzzled him, and he didn't like that one bit. Nor did he like where she worked or where she lived.

He had to do something soon.

When he'd arrived in Denver at the beginning of the week, he'd had no trouble tracking her down. The first night he'd come to the lounge, he'd planned to talk to her. Intuition had kept him quiet. Instead, he'd watched her, trying to gauge the type of woman she was.

He'd done his homework, learning she was twenty-eight, that she dabbled in pottery and had once taken a class in archaeology. He decided she either lacked drive and ambition or was spending an extended time finding herself. He found neither of those possibilities admirable.

He knew Carly Rochelle Mitchell wore too many hats. Overworked, she poured twenty-six hours of living into a twenty-four-hour day.

While watching her work, he'd noted that she moved fast around tables. Obviously, she wasn't lazy. She smiled a lot and laughed easily. She charmed customers with a breezy tone, a candid look, a natural friendliness.

A whisper of a woman, her lithe body was almost boyish. She possessed a flawless, pale complexion with a pert nose and a stubborn chin. He'd not only seen understated sensuality but had also felt it. During a fleeting second, as if taunting him, she'd swept past his table offering him a hint of a flowery scent that had aroused thoughts of a spring evening.

He'd seen a woman with the charm to incite duels if she'd been born a century ago. He'd seen a woman who could effortlessly dazzle a man. But none of that disturbed Alex. He never allowed emotion to interfere with his goals.

Carly hated Tuesdays. It was the one day a week when her class in art and design at the nearby college got out so late that she had barely an hour before she had to be at work. That meant only minutes with Billy.

At the third floor of her building, she shouted a hello to an elderly woman with a hearing problem, then charged up the next flight of stairs to her door.

Breezing into her apartment, she dumped her books on the table she'd bought at a thrift store and had refinished, grabbed her bag with her costume and scurried out of the apartment and down one flight of steps.

With a quick knock on Miriam's door, she rushed inside. His dark hair mussed from a nap, his feet and hands in motion, Billy squealed at her from the high chair. His face was smeared with something sticky and yellow; Carly assumed it was applesauce. A kiss on his cheek verified her guess. Taking a chair next to him, she laughed as he placed a sticky finger on her nose. "You are a mess."

As if she'd told him differently, he giggled with delight.

At the stove, Miriam poured a cup of coffee. A small, middle-aged woman, she was a godsend, baby-sitting for little pay while assuring Carly it was her pleasure to take care of Billy. "Have a sip of coffee," she said. "And I'll finish that."

"I have time," Carly assured Miriam, though she knew she would have to run all the way to get to work on time. "I'll finish feeding him." She dipped a spoon into the jar of applesauce on Billy's tray.

Smiling at her, Miriam bobbed her head. "You do what my mother used to call burning the candle at both ends."

The plight of all single mothers. "I manage." She stared at the coffee cup Miriam insistently held out to her. The caffeine wouldn't hurt, she decided. Usually, she avoided drinking more than a cup or two, but Tuesdays required more energy. She accepted the cup, sipped quickly, then concentrated on Billy again.

An accomplished babbler, he played out a string of sounds while grabbing at her hand for the spoon.

"I know you manage," Miriam said, her back to Carly now as she puttered around the kitchen. "Quite well, too. But you need some time for yourself."

With a half laugh, Carly lifted a shoulder.

"Did you eat?" Miriam asked her.

"I'll grab something." While Carly watched Billy's bow-shaped mouth open in anticipation of the spoon, she heard Miriam clucking behind her. Life wasn't as complicated as Miriam thought. "Do what you have to do" was Carly's motto.

She scraped the bottom of the jar and spooned the last of the applesauce into Billy's mouth. With a damp cloth, she dabbed his face clean, then gave him a quick kiss. This was the part she hated most. Leaving him. If she had any complaint in life—and she didn't have many—it was not being able to spend more time with him. "Got to go."

Miriam stood by the door. "Here."

Carly stared at the cellophane-wrapped sandwich in Miriam's hand. "Miriam, you didn't—"

"Have to. I know. It's ham and cheese. Eat it now."

"I will. While I walk. Thank you," she said and dashed out the door.

She ran the moment her sneakered feet hit the sidewalk. At a red light, she unwrapped the sandwich and munched on half of it. The other half she dropped into her purse as the light changed.

By the time she'd shimmied into her costume, she had one minute to spare. She sent an impatient-looking Roland a cheery hello in passing and geared up for a busy night as a group of conventioneers from the hotel restaurant wandered into the lounge.

Before ten o'clock Carly's adrenaline pumped, triggered by one man's constant stare. No, he wasn't just staring. His deep-set eyes were scrutinizing her. Enough, she finally decided. Call it a stubborn streak or an ornery one, but she would go nose-to-nose with him if necessary. She planned to find out now why he'd followed her last night.

Feeling knots in her shoulders, she rolled them slightly. She was already having a terrible night. Twice, she'd messed up orders because of him, because she couldn't think about anyone else.

A tray in her hand, Renee grumbled in Carly's ear, "He just left. As usual, one drink and then he leaves."

"He's gone?" Carly swung around for verification.

"Yes, he's gone. What's going on?" Renee inclined her head questioningly. "He never took his eyes off you. If I were you, I'd be thrilled, except I know he hasn't said a word to you. And *that* gives me the creeps."

"Ditto. I wish I knew what he wanted. But whatever it is, I don't like it." More at ease now, Carly delivered a smile to new customers and took their orders, then bantered with others. Though she stared into the faces of strangers, one man's face lingered in her mind.

A while later, tired and drained from underlying tension, she was ready to go home. She surveyed the room, her gaze stopping at the table where he'd sat. What if he followed her again? "Vince." She waited until the bartender looked up from wiping off the bar. "Could I ask a favor?"

He presented his best anything-you-want look. With his dark good looks, he often attracted women who willingly spent money on drinks just to engage in conversation with him. They were wasting their time. Happily married and awaiting fatherhood, he was true to his wife.

Carly laughed in response to his flirtatious expression.

"What favor?"

"There's a guy here who I think followed me last night."

"Can't blame him," he said, smiling.

Carly didn't return it. Vince teased a lot, and she usually went along with his good humor, but not this time.

"Hey, this is serious?"

"Very. I don't know what he wants."

"Which guy?" he asked, inclining his head to scan the few stragglers who hadn't left yet.

"He was the one at table eight. He's not there now. He left a while ago, but—"

"Why don't I walk you home, just to be on the safe side," he volunteered as she'd hoped.

"I'd appreciate that, Vince."

Half an hour later, Carly felt some of the evening's tension easing. She listened to Vince's humorous stories about the birthing class he and his wife, Joanne, had attended. Carly laughed with him, but she couldn't totally relax as they walked.

She hated the need to keep glancing around for one man and hoping she didn't see him.

"There's no one behind us," Vince said as she looked back yet again.

"I'm probably being silly."

"If he keeps bugging you, call the cops."

That was something she would have to think about. She didn't like getting anyone in trouble. And whoever he was, he seemed to have stopped trailing her.

Reaching the corner of her street, she noticed an approaching bus that was half a block away. At two in the morning, if Vince missed that bus, he would have to wait for another half hour. "Go home now."

"I'll walk you the rest of the way."

Feeling foolish, Carly offered him a quick smile. "Thank you for walking me, but I'm fine."

"I could wait here until you reach your building."

"No, go home. Your wife's due any minute. She might need you. And there's a bus coming. Thank you for walking me this far."

He gave her arm an affectionate squeeze. "Anytime," he assured her in brotherly fashion and sprinted across the street to reach the corner before the bus.

Her thoughts on sleep, Carly retrieved her keys from the bottom of her shoulder bag. It was footsteps behind her that swept away her relaxed mood. Sensation skittered through her like a warning, even before she made herself look back.

He stood a few feet away beneath the light of a street lamp. "Can we talk?"

Whatever he wanted didn't matter. She couldn't afford to get mugged or attacked and end up in the hospital. Who would take care of Billy? All he had was her.

Carly quickened her stride to a clipped pace and bolted up the few steps of her building. She could hear him following her. Only when her finger was poised on Miriam's buzzer did she whirl around to face him. "Who are you?"

He halted at the bottom of the stoop. "Alex Kane."

Beneath the faint light, she saw the frown in his eyes deepen. "What do you want?" she asked.

"My son," he said so softly that she barely heard him.

"What?"

With a subtle shift of his body, he seemed to move closer. "You have my son."

Chapter Two

A nut. She wasn't prepared for that. A mugger or a panhandler she knew how to handle. But this man was talking about Billy. Suddenly frightened beyond what she'd ever felt, Carly pushed Miriam's buzzer so she wouldn't have to take the time with her key.

"Who is it?" Miriam asked.

"Me, Carly. Open up, please," she yelled into the voice box. Her hand behind her, she twisted the doorknob in unison with the sound of the buzzer.

Shoving open the door with her back, she met the man's intense stare only for a second, then scurried in. Her heart banged at the wall of her chest as she raced up the first flight of steps. She dared one look at the glass door. He was gone. Her legs unsteady, she sagged against the wall.

Above her, Miriam called out, "Carly, are you all right?"

"Fine," she managed to say between shaky breaths. But she wasn't. She was scared. Petrified.

Somehow, she hid her fear from Miriam. Stepping into her apartment minutes later, Carly gripped Billy tightly. With his head against her chest, his soft hair tickled the underside of her chin. She should put him to bed, but for a few seconds, she wanted, needed, to hold him close.

This is all a mistake, she told herself. He—Alex Kane—had the wrong woman, the wrong child. He'd simply made a mistake. She kept that thought in her mind as she carried Billy to bed and tucked him in, as she undressed, as she stared for hours at the dark ceiling.

"He said you have his son?" Renee asked on a yawn.

Six in the morning bordered on a ridiculous time to call anyone, but Carly needed to talk to someone. "Yes," she answered, coiling the telephone cord around her finger.

"He really said that?" Renee asked in astonishment, sounding suddenly very awake.

"I already told you. Yes, he did."

"What kind of weirdo is he?"

"I don't know. We both know he's lying. He couldn't be Billy's father."

Renee was silent, an oddity for her. "Are you sure?"

No, how could she be? After all, Billy was adopted. What if he was Billy's father? Oh, God, she couldn't lose him. So much had been taken from her already.

Curiosity edged Renee's voice. "What are you going to do?"

Carly had been asking herself that all night. "I suppose I have to talk to him."

"Why do you have to?"

"I don't think he'll leave me alone until I do. I've thought about this. He must be mistaken." To believe anything else promised thoughts that were more frightening. "Or insane."

By the time she uttered a goodbye to Renee, she felt steadier. She would talk to him, clear up the misunderstanding and get him out of her life. She hoped.

Needing contact with Billy, she stepped close to his crib and found he'd kicked off the blanket. After covering him and giving him a kiss, she dressed quickly and put on a pair of earrings that fascinated Billy.

More doubts fluttered in her mind as she recalled how determined Alex Kane had sounded. She'd already pegged him as a man used to power plays. Self-assured. Intimidating. When he'd been a stranger at Top Hat, she'd been able to ignore him, almost. How could she now? He was talking about someone precious to her, someone who gave her life direction, someone she loved so much she would die for him.

What if Alex Kane really was Billy's father? As she walked into the kitchen, her stomach somersaulted with the idea. Though caffeine might not help the situation, the dark brew would settle her nerves. She poured a cup and cradled it to warm suddenly cold hands, then nearly dropped it when the buzzer sounded.

None of her friends would dare visit her at seven in the morning. It was him. She knew that even before she heard his voice. "Come up," Carly said because she believed to live in fear was worse than facing it. "Apartment 401."

A hand on the doorknob, she geared up for some uncomfortable moments before opening the door.

He looked different. She'd almost begun to believe he slept in his suit. It seemed so normal to see him wearing one. Yet he looked so right now, too, dressed in tight, faded jeans and a midnight blue polo shirt. Amazingly, he looked quite comfortable and natural. "Mr. Kane." It was then that she saw his sneakers. Snow-white without a smudge on them. "Come in," she said, certain they would buck heads within seconds.

One step inside and Alex knew he hadn't made a mistake about his son needing his steadying influence in his life. First, she hadn't even questioned him before letting him in. Weren't women taught to be cautious? Second, she dressed weird, at least in comparison to the fashion-plate women he'd become accustomed to.

Inch-long earrings that resembled lizards swayed with the slightest movement of her head. Her oversize blouse had the strangest design he'd ever seen. Patches of vivid colors—searing oranges and eye-squinting pinks and reds—seemed to run together. Nearly bleached-white snug jeans showed off her legs almost as well as the brief costume she wore at work. Her shiny hair, a color that reminded him of a field of wheat, was tousled. He would call it messy. Barefoot, she'd painted her toenails hot-pink.

He swept a slow appraising look around the room. It, too, was a riot of color. Nothing matched, from the bright pink cabinet to the sea green sofa. Yet, if he was honest, he would admit everything seemed to look good together.

Alex scowled at the thought and the mess in a corner of her kitchen. Shelves contained various-shaped pots. He skimmed what he assumed was a potter's work area—the buckets, scales, sponges, brushes, potter's wheel. Not for the first time, he decided that his son would live in chaos with this woman. "I'm glad you agreed to talk to me."

"I only have a few moments," Carly said in a tone that carried no welcome. "What did you mean when you said I have your son?"

Alex wasn't in the mood for niceties, either. "I'm the boy's birth father," he announced, noting the clean kitchen counter where she'd lined up baby bottles.

Carly thought her legs would buckle. Her heart pounding, she fought to gather her thoughts. "What are you talking about?"

His stare never wavered. "I'm the boy's birth father," he repeated.

Though she held panic at bay, irritation spiraled through her like a whirlwind. "The *boy* has a name. William—Billy."

"Billy," he repeated as if testing the name. "I learned your brother, Randall, and his wife, Emily, adopted him, but they'd moved from San Francisco. Now, I appreciate the care you've been giving to him—"

Carly fought the unexpected surge of grief and cut in, "Just a minute." Did he really think he could simply walk in and take Billy from her? No way was she going to take his word as fact. "What proof do you have?"

"Proof?"

He seemed astonished that she hadn't simply accepted his claim. "Yes, I want proof."

His disturbing gaze, cool and deciphering, fixed on her. "Of course you would."

With two fingers, he rubbed his forehead in a way that assured her he wasn't as calm and composed as he pretended.

"I should have brought the birth certificate with me." Such an oversight on his part was uncharacteristic, but Alex had been distracted, thinking only about seeing the child that was his. "I'll be back." He took a step, then stilled. Cynically he wondered if she'd take off the moment he disappeared from sight. "What guarantee do I have that you'll be here when I get back?"

Slipping her fingers into the small pockets of her jeans, Carly bristled. "I guess you'll just have to trust me."

Alex never trusted easily. "Don't take off."

He was not likable, she decided, and nearly slammed the door at his back.

"Proof," Alex said half an hour later, standing in her doorway and holding a sheet of paper in front of her nose.

Carly gripped Billy tighter, not unaware of the curious visual exchange between him and Alex Kane. With a sinking feeling of dread, she read the names on the birth certificate. "Amanda Devereau and Alexander Kane."

Alex couldn't take his eyes off the boy. Though there had been only a few photos of himself as a child, he'd seen one. The boy before him resembled that child. *My son.* The words still seemed strange to him. Chubby-faced with wide green eyes, the baby pressed his dark head into the soft curve of her neck, but kept staring at

Alex curiously. "Do you want to see identification? A driver's license or...?"

Carly shifted Billy to her other arm, unconsciously placing more distance between him and the man at her door. "That's not necessary. But I do have to verify that this is legitimate."

Alex noticed that she wore shoes now, lemon yellow sneakers. "It has the state seal of California on it."

"Yes, I noticed." She reached forward to take the document. "Give it to me, and I'll—"

Alex snatched the paper back. "Do I look stupid? If I give this to you, I have no proof."

Stalemate. For a long moment, they simply stared each other down. Carly sighed at the ridiculousness of the moment. "I need to take the birth certificate to my lawyer."

That seemed logical to Alex. "Fine," he answered, not fazed by the irritation in her tone. "I'll drive."

The nod from her lawyer forty-five minutes later sank Carly's heart. Only for a second. Quickly she combated any inkling of defeat. That he'd verified the authenticity of the birth certificate meant nothing. "We haven't checked the footprints yet," she announced, hurrying outside.

Alex fell in step beside her. He admired her never-give-up attitude. The same trait had controlled him through his youth, and when he'd begun looking for his son. For months, he'd searched for what he'd felt was his but that had been stolen from him.

As the boy in her arms grinned, clearly delighted to touch the earring dangling close to his fingers, something unfamiliar inched its way inside Alex. He now saw more than a miniature version of himself; he saw the child, imagined the person Billy would become. His son. They'd just been words before this, an intangible in Alex's mind. But the boy was real, a little person who smiled and laughed, who squirmed in the woman's arms, and Alex suddenly wanted to hold him. He knew better than to ask. She maintained a possessive grip on the boy as if keeping him safe from danger.

Hours later, the disturbing knot in Carly's stomach coiled tighter. As tears smarted her eyes, she blinked them away. Before her was proof. Billy's footprints on a sheet of paper perfectly matched the ones on the birth certificate.

Panic rushing in on her, she kept an eye on Billy in the back seat while they drove to her apartment. The moment the car stopped, she took Billy out of the car seat and almost ran to reach her apartment building. It was a childish action. Nothing would help, not even running from the man behind her. Alex Kane wouldn't leave her alone. As she reached the bottom step of the stoop outside the building, she noted that his long legs were steadily closing the distance between them.

Carly cuddled Billy so tightly to her that he squirmed. "I'm sorry," she whispered and kissed his temple. "It's just that I love you so much." She went up the stairs to the fourth floor, unlocked her apartment door, but didn't bother to close it. Whether she wanted company or not, she sensed she would have it, anyway.

After placing Billy in his high chair, she set a pan of water on a burner. She dodged the emotions muddling her mind. She had to think clearly. She needed a miracle.

Behind her, she heard the squeak of a floorboard then the click of the door closing. For a few more minutes, she strove for normalcy, reaching into a cupboard for a baby jar of peaches and setting a bottle to warm in the heated water. She wanted to turn back the clock and pretend none of this had happened.

One man insisted differently. "Now, it's time to talk," he said curtly.

Carly shot a look of irritation at him. That tone might work on others, but not her. "And I have a child to feed," she countered. What she wanted to do was yell at him to leave. He was disrupting her life. He was scaring her. "If you wanted him before, why did you ever let him go?" she asked almost challengingly.

"I didn't know about him." Vividly, Alex recalled the turmoil that had swept into his life when he'd learned he was a father.

"Billy's seven months old." Carly tied a bib at the back of Billy's neck. "Why did you wait so long?"

Though she hadn't offered him a seat, Alex dropped to a chair close to Billy. Lightly he brushed a finger across one of the baby's small hands. It felt rubbery, softer than the most sensuous skin he'd ever touched. "It's taken me this long to locate him." He hunched forward as his son offered him a toothless grin. "I searched San Francisco to locate your brother, then learned he'd moved."

That he spoke in a less combative tone made Carly look at him. Not prone to anxiety around strangers, Billy had curled his fingers around one of Alex's. "My brother got a new job weeks after the adoption." Carly sprinkled drops from the baby bottle on the underside of her wrist. "Do you live there?" she asked, stalling for time while she mentally hunted for a way to get this man out of her life.

"Near it." Her civil tone encouraged Alex, but he wasn't fooled by it. Her back remained rigidly straight. "As the birth father, the Department of Health Services in Utah where she had the baby notified me. That's when I first learned about him. I had thirty days to register a claim of paternity. Which I did. Then it got more complicated. It took me all this time to locate him."

Just then, Billy let out an impatient wail, whipping Carly around. At the droning serenade, Alex gave her an I'm-innocent-look that might have been endearing under different circumstances. "How did you get the birth certificate?"

Alex was still marveling at his son's lung power. "From the baby's mother. She gave it to me when I confronted her," he said as she sat before his son with his food. Alex watched Billy's bow-shaped mouth greedily close over the spoon of fruit.

Carly nibbled at her bottom lip. Is that what this was all about? Did Billy's birth mother want him back?

"As I said, I realize you've cared for him since..." Not totally insensitive, Alex paused, mindful she'd lost a brother and could still be grieving. "Look, I'm sure you've had a difficult time," he went on, choosing a different path. "And I appreciate the care you've given Billy."

With effort, Carly blocked the painful memory of losing Randy and Emily. "I wasn't doing you a favor."

"In a way, you have been."

Pinned by the frown in his eyes, Carly took a ragged breath. She knew now what bothered her most about him. He carried the same edge of influence she'd been surrounded by while growing up. People with power wore their arrogance like badges. Years ago, she'd never intimidated well. She didn't plan to start now. It was time to set him straight. "According to a legal document—their will—I'm his guardian."

"For the moment," he said with such certainty that she knew if she'd been standing, her legs would have buckled. "I don't care about that paper. He's *my* son."

It pained her, but she had to face the truth. Alex Kane was Billy's father. Billy's babyish features bore a hint of Alex's nose and mouth. Eyes, more green than brown, widened every time he opened his mouth for the spoon. Yet, she wanted to scream, *He's not yours. He's mine.* She loved Billy; she cared for him. She would die without him.

Alex watched her blink several times in the manner of someone fighting tears. Hell, this was worse than he'd expected. After he'd learned of the adoptive parents' deaths, he'd been more desperate to find his son, unsure what had happened to him. When he'd found out the adoptive father's sister had him, he'd felt a touch of relief. Then, he'd learned more about her.

She'd left San Francisco at nineteen, and for a year, she'd lived in some wacky artist's apartment in Seattle. Whether the man had been her lover or not hadn't mattered to Alex. When her brother had moved to Denver, she'd left Seattle and had joined him.

She seemed flighty and hardly the personification of motherhood. According to the facts he'd been able to uncover about her past, she'd earned a living selling flowers on a street corner and waiting tables at a biker's grill. Before meeting her, he'd half expected to find her decorated from neck to foot with tattoos. Instead, she worked as a cocktail waitress at a high-class hotel lounge.

At the moment, though, she didn't seem so flaky. She looked fragile, breakable, and Alex had a lousy taste in his mouth as he acknowledged he was the one who would break her. Topping that, he had a hell of a desire to put his arms around her and tell her that everything would be okay. But, of course, it wouldn't be. By the loving look in her eyes when she stared at his son, Alex knew he was going to hurt her. He was going to make her cry.

While she carried Billy into the other room, Alex ambled over to the coffeepot. He was dying for a cup of coffee. Strong coffee. He sneaked a look in her refrigerator—for his son's sake, he reasoned. The shelves were sparsely filled. Besides a bottle of orange juice, milk and several baby-food jars, she had green Jell-O and a ready-made salad.

Quietly he closed the fridge door, then opened a cupboard in search of a cup. An overabundance of canned goods lined a shelf. She seemed to have a propensity for chili, peanut-butter-and-jelly sandwiches and snacks suitable for a ten-year-old's tastes.

In the next cupboard, he found the cups and poured himself some coffee. With caution, he sipped the steaming brew. On a wall above the stove, she'd hung a calendar, one of those cutesy kinds with photos of puppies.

It took only minutes to sense that she would rebel against everything he'd struggled to have. Free spirits and workaholics rarely found common ground.

Somehow, he had to penetrate her whimsical world and bring her back to reality. The boy was his. Alex didn't plan to wait around for her to accept that.

In another week, he was supposed to formulate Webb Electronics Corporation's long-term operations strategy for a new telecommunications division they'd recently purchased. Already he'd been away from his job too long. His work had always been everything to him. As chief executive of operations, he couldn't afford to spend a lot of time away. Before he'd left California, hints had circulated around the building that he might be named the corporation's new CEO. Alexander Kane, a man who'd dragged himself out of the south side of Chicago, was a step away from reaching his goal. He couldn't let that go. But he couldn't abandon his son, either.

Carly tucked Billy into bed and stalled a moment, needing a clear mind before she returned to the living room. She'd gotten through plenty before by being optimistic. She needed to rouse some of that uplifting confidence now. But what if... ? No, she wouldn't let herself consider any what ifs.

Lovingly, she ran a hand over Billy's head. "Me and the Unsinkable Molly Brown are from the same mold," she assured her sleeping nephew.

She was going to win.

Chapter Three

Carly marched back into the living room, prepared to face the problem head-on. So far, she'd made one mistake. After Alex Kane had announced who he was, she'd expected time to mull over what was happening. With the day off, she'd planned to take Billy to the park, browse in the thrift shop, enjoy the day. And tonight, she would do the laundry.

None of that mattered now, and she couldn't afford to make another mistake, believing he would give her time. Clearly, he was a man of action, one of those quick-on-his-feet, decisive kinds.

She noticed he'd found the coffee, and looked amazingly comfortable in *her* kitchen while she felt displaced. "What is she like?" Carly asked, trying to understand what the woman had had to cope with, why she'd felt she'd had no choice but to give up her child.

Puzzlement etched a faint line in his forehead. "Who?"

"His mother."

Resting his backside against the kitchen counter, Alex considered her question a little odd since he was the one who wanted the boy, not his mother. "She's quite brilliant."

But of course. Carly should have guessed that. He probably considered his time too valuable to waste on someone who wasn't, but she didn't think the woman was so smart. She'd given up Billy.

"She's a concert pianist. She's been playing since she was four, a child protégée of Vansourn," he said as if mentioning the world-famous pianist was a sufficient explanation.

But none of what he said meant diddly to Carly. "And?"

"And?" he repeated, looking confused once more.

"Why did she give up her baby?"

"I told you why."

Carly couldn't keep the snideness out of her voice. "Because she can play the piano."

Alex allowed his gaze to wander to her mouth. Despite her bold outfit, she wore only a dash of lipstick. A touch too wide for the small face, her lips carried a hint of a smile even when a frown clouded her eyes. "I don't think we're communicating," he said quietly.

Emotion had taken control of her. "Oh, we're communicating just fine."

"Let me explain."

Carly willed down her anger and bent over to retrieve one of Billy's toys from the floor.

Her blouse veed, offering a shadowy hint of breast. Mentally, Alex swore at the sudden heating of his blood. What he couldn't afford was *that* kind of distraction. "She had a career, a brilliant one."

There was that word *brilliant* again, Carly mused.

"She tours with some of the finest symphonies. She's performed before royalty."

"Bottom line," Carly insisted, standing and turning away to drop the toy in a small box in the kitchen. "Has she decided now that motherhood might be more fulfilling?"

Alex nudged his attention from the strain of denim across her backside. "No," he answered louder than he intended because she was having an annoying effect on him.

Carly's heartbeat remained at its quickened beat even though the knot in her stomach uncoiled. The fear gripping her since he'd made his announcement yesterday lessened. "She doesn't want him?"

"No, she doesn't."

She noted he avoided her eyes, as if having to make such an admission made him uncomfortable. Too bad, she thought. He'd made her life a living hell for the past day. He deserved some discomfort, too.

"She's a good woman. Really," Alex said because he believed that to be true. Amanda had never wanted marriage or a family. Music was her life. She was dedicated to it, even obsessed with it. Lacking even a smidgen of maternal instinct, she'd acted wisely by not keeping their son. What he still couldn't come to terms with is that she hadn't told him about the child, that she'd made a decision to give him up for adoption without considering if he'd want his son.

"But a kid with sticky fingers and smelly diapers didn't fit into her life." Carly didn't attempt to veil her disgust at what some people believed took priority above a child. Even as she was grateful the birth mother didn't want Billy, she felt angry that the woman could shun a little boy who was so precious.

"I can see you're upset, but we need to talk calmly."

Carly didn't want to talk to him anymore. She'd lost so much. Billy was her child now. They were bonded by a night of agony when he'd had an ear infection, by the purple giraffe he couldn't sleep without, by moments as simple as him bubbling beets back at her.

His well-being propelled her through every minute of hard work. Before he'd become her responsibility, she'd drifted through life. Since her world had narrowed to him and her, she'd settled down. She'd set goals, planned for their future. Nothing was easy, but she managed to attend school, hold down a job, make her pottery and provide him with the love and care he deserved. She had to make his father understand. "He's been with me since he was two months old, since my brother and his wife died." The words nearly caught in her throat. They'd been so happy. Almost instantly, her brother had fallen in love with Emily. They'd waited for years for a child. Finally, after dozens of tests, they'd adopted.

"We've been blessed," Randy used to say.

He and Emily had endured three difficult years of waiting for the adoption that would give them a child. Then miraculously, they'd gotten a newborn. They'd been so happy, so filled with dreams of the future.

Without warning, Carly felt aching grief sneak in, trying to engulf her as it had for months. This time, she avoided its grip—had to. If she let emotion take over, she would be weaker. She needed all the strength she could muster at the moment. "They were killed in a small-plane crash." She offered her back to him to pour herself a cup of coffee. "My brother worked as a consultant for a pharmaceutical firm. Emily nearly didn't go with him to Salt Lake, but it was supposed to be only for the weekend, so they left Billy with me. They'd laughed, teasing each other about a second honeymoon." Raising her head, Carly managed a cheerless smile. "That was a private joke between them, because they'd never had the first."

"I'm sorry." Alex caught a glimpse of how lost she'd been, of the sadness she'd survived. "That must have been a devastating time for you."

His sensitivity to what she'd felt surprised her. Her brother had been all she'd had. "Billy made the difference for me," Carly answered softly. He was all she had now. All she had. "I'm the only one Billy's known since they died."

Alex couldn't think of a way to make his next words less painful to her. "His mother gave him away. I didn't," he felt compelled to remind her. "I want him."

Carly's head jerked up. "I told you that my brother and his wife left a will naming me as his guardian." While she was shaking inside, he seemed so calm. She fought her own fear. "What if one day you decide you don't want him, or the birth mother changes her mind and decides she made a mistake and she wants him? Do you know what that would do to him? Do you know what your taking him from me will do?"

"I can assure you—"

"You can offer me no assurances unless you're willing to leave him right where he is. I'm not going to agree to anything else."

Alex abandoned the idea of steamrolling her. He'd already noticed the prideful squaring of her shoulders, the stubborn tilt of her chin. "It's clear you're struggling. Who takes care of him while you're at work?"

Carly was no fool. He was using a different approach. She'd already guessed where he was heading. "A neighbor, Miriam Bonwick, watches him at night when I'm working and the couple of hours a week when I have class. But this is all temporary. I'm a potter. I plan to open my own shop."

A chance in a million, Alex assumed, pegging her as a full-fledged dreamer. "Years from now."

At the rate she was saving money, Carly thought even a decade from now was too optimistic.

"So besides being short on time, you're in need of money."

Here it comes, Carly mused.

"There is an easy solution to this. I could help financially. Without the boy—Billy to take care of—"

Anger rose so swiftly in her, she swayed with it. "I'm not interested in...help," she interrupted. "I don't need it." Years ago, she'd made that decision. She had relatives who, in their own well-meaning way, might have offered help, but they would have also imposed constraints on her. She preferred standing alone if it meant being free from others' conditions.

Alex couldn't help admiring her obstinacy. He believed if a person wanted something, he should be willing to fight for it. "I understand your feelings, but you're not being sensible."

He couldn't know those were the worst words he could have said to her. How many times had her aunt used those same words? "Oh, really?"

Alex pushed away from the counter. That had definitely been the wrong thing to say. "You're single." *And a knockout.* He frowned at the thought. He couldn't afford to let this slip of a woman or his awareness of her divert him from his goal.

"I got the impression you were, too."

"That's different."

Carly would have laughed if she wasn't so scared.

Alex eyed the huge Snoopy piggy bank on the top of her refrigerator. "You're a practical woman, aren't you?"

In a mocking manner, Carly arched an eyebrow. "But not too sensible. Isn't that what you said?"

Alex had gauged himself for this moment. Timing was everything. "I don't believe you're prepared for a court battle."

Those words aroused Carly's worst fear. If they went to court, Billy might be taken away from her. Alex had the edge of being Billy's natural father, of providing the child with a better life. At least, on the surface, it would look that way.

"I can provide for him in a way you can't."

But do you love him? Carly wanted to ask. *I love him.* How would she go on with her life without Billy? He'd had a place in her heart from the moment her brother and his wife had brought their son home. "Please," she said, unable to keep her fear at bay any longer. "You can't just walk in here and take him. He'll be confused."

"He's a baby," Alex retorted, facing her.

Clearly, the man didn't understand children. "And how will you care for him?"

Alex had given little thought to what he would do once he'd found his son. All that had mattered was finding him. "I can hire a nanny. I have the resources."

Carly sighed. Wasn't that always the way of life for a child born into affluence? "You're right. I can't match your dollar value," she admitted. "But there's one thing I can do for Billy that you can't."

Alex hadn't expected this much opposition. "What's that?"

"I can take care of him. I'll bet you don't know a thing about caring for a baby."

She had him there.

By his expression, Carly knew she'd made her point, so she drove it home. "What about doctor's appointments? You'll have to take him to those. And do you realize that a baby ties you down? He'll slow down your social life."

Alex curtailed his own, usually. Work came first, always.

"You'll have to budget time for doctors and school conferences and—and Little League."

With a turn away to set down his cup, he said offhandedly, "That's many years from now." Actually, he was more concerned with how to deal with the next diaper change.

Carly folded a dish towel to keep her hands from shaking. "All right. Then how will you deal with childhood diseases?"

To his way of thinking, that question was one of her easier ones. "Vaccinations."

Carly couldn't believe he narrowed everything down to such simple facts. "Except for chicken pox," she decided to remind him.

Out the window, Alex saw two boys riding bikes on the sidewalk. How difficult could it be to raise a child? Millions of people did it. "I can handle a bout with a child's illness."

So smug, Carly mused. He thinks everything is so easy. Just wait, she wanted to say. "Also, children get colds. All the time."

Alex faced her with a look that had shut down some mightier opponents than her, but he'd added her list of problems to the complications he'd already anticipated. While she'd been feeding his son, he'd felt an uneasiness gnawing at him because he knew he wasn't knowledgeable enough to care for a baby. What he knew about were power struggles and executive game playing. "Really, this isn't changing my mind."

No, Carly could see it wasn't. Determination had punctuated his words. She would guess he was uncompromising when he thought he was right, which was probably always. "Unlike you, I can find a job that meshes with being a mother. So far, I have single-handedly and successfully managed that. I've proven I can take care of Billy by myself."

Again, silence hung in the air as their gazes clashed. They weren't making progress. Two stubborn people who lived different life-styles, who viewed life differently, probably never would. "Did you actually think I'd just let you take him?" Carly asked.

Alex supposed he had. He'd assumed since she wasn't the one who'd done the adopting, since she was single and obviously used to living her life by a loose set of rules, that she would be, if not pleased, then relieved to no longer have the responsibilities of raising a child.

Determined, Carly angled up her chin. "You're right about my not having a lot of money, but if fighting you is the only way I can keep Billy, then I will."

Alex weighed his options. He'd asked her to be rational. Amazingly, she was making a lot of sense. He had a job, one he couldn't ignore, but he wanted his son. If she wouldn't give up the boy, he might never get back home. Despite what he'd said, he didn't have the time for a court battle. In his mind, there was only one other way. "I've come up with a solution."

Turning to the sink to rinse out a dish, Carly could think of no solution he would favor that she would agree to.

More certain now of the direction he planned to take with her, Alex lounged against the kitchen counter. "I'm going to make a suggestion that I think will be acceptable to you."

Carly doubted that.

"Do you believe in compromise?"

She leveled a wary look at him. "I don't see how we can compromise about this."

"Sure we can. All you have to do is come with me to California."

That won her full attention. Speechless, a rarity for her, she sank onto the closest chair and shut her gaping mouth while she tried to understand. "What exactly are you proposing?"

It took effort for Alex not to smile. "Strictly business," he assured her.

Carly didn't understand. "Go to California? Why? Why are you suggesting this?"

Alex moved closer because he wanted to bridge more than the distance between them. Distractedly, something churned within him as he caught the scent of lemon in her hair. "I would think that's obvious. Because of Billy. He's used to you. If you take care of him for me, I'll help you get your shop."

Flabbergasted by his suggestion, Carly felt her heart skip. He was offering her a chance to succeed, to work at what she loved. But most of all, she was being offered a way to stay with Billy. She would do anything for him. Anything. But some precautions needed to be considered. "I don't know anything about you."

Alex sensed the scale tipping his way. "I'm thirty-five. Before my position at Webb Electronics Corporation, I was vice president of marketing for a computer software firm."

Facts meant nothing. Carly needed to know about him as a person. A sane woman didn't accept such an offer from a stranger. "But are you crazy?"

A faint flush had crept into her cheeks. She looked lovely. No other word came to mind to describe her. Alex swore mentally. He couldn't keep getting sidetracked. "What do you want?" he asked because of the doubt still in her eyes. "References?"

Carly sent him a deadly serious look. "As a matter of fact, I do."

"You're serious?"

The way he kept studying her made her uneasy. "Yes, I am."

His lips stretched in a slow smile that was more disruptive than calming to her. "Okay. I'll give them to you. Check them out while you're packing."

"Wait a minute." No longer numbed by the fear of having Billy whisked away, Carly laughed. "You want me to pack up, sublease my apartment and just take off?"

Alex couldn't understand the problem. From what he'd learned about her, she seemed inclined to do that, anyway. "I got the impression there wasn't anyone significantly important to you here."

More humor rose in Carly. What an emotionless way to discuss the love of someone's life.

He inclined his head. "Is that a problem?" he asked.

"No." Since she'd become Billy's guardian, she'd given little thought to the lack of a love interest in her life. "But there are other problems."

"What?" Impatience seeped into his voice. "If you're concerned about subleasing, I'll work something out with the apartment manager."

Carly's head spun. Though impulsive occasionally, she wasn't foolish. "I have to think about it," she said, but she'd already considered a custody battle. Not having the money to fight him, she knew she would lose.

"Why?" he demanded. "You either want to be with the boy or you don't."

She hadn't underestimated him, Carly realized. He knew how to cut at a person with precision accuracy. "There are a lot of questions. Like, would I have trouble finding a place to live?"

What she interpreted as growing impatience deepened his frown. "I assumed you realized that would be no problem."

Her back stiffened at the trace of arrogance in his voice.

"You'll live at my house," Alex said simply.

Carly was sure she'd misunderstood him. "What did you say?"

"You'll live with me."

She laughed then. "Oh, you definitely need to rest." At his deadpan look, indignation rose within her. "I don't know what you're thinking. But just because I work as a cocktail waitress doesn't mean I'm easy."

Alex snorted a laugh. *Easy.* She was far from it. She'd already revealed an iron will and obstinacy that he couldn't recall facing since he'd set up production in a foreign country with its labor and cultural differences. "In my house. Not in my bed," he clarified. Though she wasn't his type, he had to admit she was stunning in a wholesome way. "You'd even have a chaperon. Dora is my cook and housekeeper."

"You really want me to move in with you?"

"My house is big enough," Alex assured her.

"But we're strangers."

A grin hiked up a corner of his lips. "Who isn't when they first meet?"

Carly stared at him in disbelief. She assumed he considered that a logical explanation. It sounded flippant to her.

"How long would it take you to get ready? A few days?"

"I didn't say yes," she reminded him.

Alex waited a second to rein in his temper. He thought he'd offered a perfectly logical solution, and she was still being difficult. "I need to go back to California in a few days. Are you going with me, or am I going to a lawyer?"

Carly drew a leveling breath to quell her anxiousness. She had no choice. "With you."

Not as confident about the outcome as he'd pretended, Alex veiled his relief. "Then can you get organized in a few days?" he asked as tension eased from his shoulders.

Organized she wasn't, except in her work. She would go crazy trying to do everything in that time, but she wouldn't admit that to him, especially him, Mr. Organization with a capital *O*. "Yes, I could do that."

"Good. We have a deal."

She felt shell-shocked. What was she doing? She hardly knew him.

Because it was natural in his business, Alex offered his hand. "I'm glad that we worked this out."

Carly stared at his hand. Before she allowed herself time to consider the insanity of this agreement, she set her hand in his to seal the deal.

Tightly, his fingers folded around hers and held them for a second—an eternity of one. Carly's breath lodged in her throat. Honest to the core, especially about her own feelings, she acknowledged the quickening of her pulse as a sensual reaction to a better-than-average-looking man. But more unsettling was how right his touch felt. She met his eyes levelly, attempting to seem undisturbed. "Did you want to say something else?"

Wispy blond strands brushed her forehead, tempting him to touch them. Alex rationalized away the urge as meaning nothing. By nature, he always liked everything in place. Even her hair seemed in opposition to his way of thinking. "I'll be by tomorrow. If you need any help, just ask."

After so many moments of feeling on the defensive, Carly couldn't pass up an opportunity to enjoy herself a little at his expense. "Well, you could scrounge around for cartons."

"Scrounge—" He didn't miss the amusement in her eyes.

"If you have time." She sent him a smile that he'd tag as spine-tingling, the kind of smile that suckered a guy in and would have him doing anything she asked.

Alex dragged his gaze away from her lips. Flashes of this softer side of her disturbed him more than the spirited one. "I'll see what I can find."

The irritation was back on his face again, Carly noted. Without another word, he went out the door. Only then did the pressure swelling in her chest finally ease.

That evening, she gave her notice at the Top Hat.

Renee had nearly fainted when she'd revealed Alex's arrangement. "Are you sure he isn't planning something funny?"

Carly doubted he had a funny bone in his body. "It's like business to him. All he wants to do is return to California with his son. I'm a complication. Therefore, he found a solution."

Renee scowled at her explanation. "That sounds so cut-and-dried."

"That's how Mr. Organization operates."

"Gorgeous but dull?"

"Exactly," Carly agreed.

Chapter Four

Bedlam. That's what Alex faced the next morning. Foolishly, he'd thought he had everything under control. Standing in the doorway of her apartment, he winced at the ear-piercing guitar music blaring from a radio on the counter. He surveyed the half-packed cartons, opened cupboards and clothes piled on the sofa.

She had no system at all.

As usual, he relied on logic to see him through. If he viewed her as a challenge, he thought, he could deal with this upheaval in his life. "I brought more cartons."

Determined to make the best of this situation, Carly summoned a smile for him. "That was thoughtful of you," she said, carrying a folded stroller toward the door.

Alex dropped the cartons he'd brought in. Politeness might work, he decided. As she flitted away then whisked back into the room with a small plastic tub and an armful of towels, he realized he'd been prepared to witness a more lackadaisical attitude toward the packing. Her energetic start pleased him, and puzzled him. Since she hardly seemed lazy, why hadn't she built a future for herself before this? He planned to find out the answer to that question, but not now. At this moment, he needed to get her organized. "You can't pack towels and silverware together," he yelled over the noise of the music.

Kneeling beside a carton, Carly reached back and flicked off the radio. "Why can't I?"

"Because they belong in two different rooms."

This was going to be more difficult than she'd anticipated. Carly had expected bossiness. A man used to taking control probably had always been a leader. No doubt it had started when he was child. He'd been the one to call the shots on the baseball or football field, the boy others looked up to and followed. What she'd been unprepared for was how much he reminded her of everything she'd escaped years ago—people who were hell-bent on what was proper.

Jumping through hoops on the command of others had never been her style, but she would make the best of whatever happened. For Billy, she had to. "I am making progress," she assured him because she'd seen the shadow of a frown in his eyes. She bounded to a stand and opened a cupboard door to reveal empty shelves. "See?"

Alex paused in running tape across the flaps of a carton. She appeared pleased, so proud of the headway she'd made, while he felt as if they were on one of those treadmills, working hard and going nowhere.

Receiving another one of his frowns, Carly wasn't sure if they would get through the packing, much less— What? What was the plan? She *was* sensible. Enough to realize they couldn't simply live together without complications. What if one of them fell in love, wanted to get married? Three definitely was a crowd.

Perhaps it was best not to look for trouble. For right now, he'd come up with a solution that allowed her to be with Billy. She would think about problems and legalities later. Standing, she stretched her back, then fished into her shoulder bag for a box of candy. "We need a break," she said and tossed several candies into her mouth.

Alex rotated a sculpture that resembled nothing he could recognize. "You just started."

Actually, she'd been busy since before dawn. "Not really. Anyway, I'm starving."

It seemed incredible to him. She'd been popping the chocolate treats in her mouth nonstop. "Don't you have any food besides those?"

Carly plopped the empty candy box into the garbage can. "The kitchen cupboards are already empty, aren't they? Since I'm moving, and I couldn't pack the food, I gave it away."

"Why would you do that?" He looked baffled. "You have to eat."

Carly frowned at him. "I thought you would be pleased that I'd accomplished something."

Was she making fun of him? Though Alex narrowed his eyes, he gave up his scowl quickly. It was having no effect on her.

"Give me a minute to get Billy ready, and we can leave to get some food."

"Leave?" Alex swiveled a look at the window and the water streaming down. "You do know it's raining, don't you?"

Carly sighed. The man made a habit of exaggerating. She doubted he'd done one spontaneous or impulsive act in his life. Even more than before, she was sure her decision to go with him was the right one, not only because of her feelings for Billy, but also for Billy's sake. Billy needed someone who would provide him with what he needed most—love and laughter.

"It's only drizzling. And I have the cutest rain outfit for Billy. Wait until you see—" Carly stopped mid-sentence as she swept a look over the packed boxes. If only she had X-ray vision. "I think it's in this box," she said, yanking up the flaps of the carton. "Nope. This has medicine-cabinet stuff. It must be this one then." She scooted to another container and ripped off the tape he'd so meticulously placed across the flaps.

Alex dragged his gaze away from her T-shirt molding to her breasts. Fools rush in, he cautioned, thinking the trite saying carried a wealth of wisdom.

"Not this one, either." Carly rummaged in another carton. "I know it's in this one."

Alex looked up from retaping the flaps on the carton she'd opened. Looking askance at the box, she brushed away strands of hair caressing her cheek. He noticed then how sun-streaked her hair was and wondered if it was as soft as it looked.

Squatting, Carly unpacked stacks of baby clothing and set them at her feet. "Here it is." She beamed, pushed to a stand and held up a bright red raincoat and hood for his approval. "Isn't this adorable?"

Alex said the obvious. "You're getting nothing done opening cartons you just packed. Why don't you label the boxes?"

Carly ignored his suggestion. "I couldn't resist it when I saw it." She received no response. She hadn't expected one.

Feet planted firmly on the floor, he scanned the chaos she'd caused while looking for the outfit and muttered something under his breath.

When they finally left the apartment, rain drizzled around them while low-hanging, gray clouds promised even more dismal weather. Alex scowled at the rain staining the tips of his sneakers, and wished he'd brought his umbrella. With his head down, he kept his eyes on his feet. He dodged a puddle; she went through it.

Wearing a bright yellow slicker, she flung the diaper bag over her shoulder. His son in her arms, she walked at a leisurely pace, as if it were a sunny day.

"I know the perfect place to eat." Carly turned eyes bright with enthusiasm on him. "Follow me."

Following anyone wasn't Alex's standard procedure. "Is it far...?" He let his words trail off and looked up in time to see her deviating to the left to open the door of a delicatessen. "Are we eating here?"

With her glance over her shoulder, he saw the laughter in her eyes. "No."

Why had he made himself a part of this cozy outing? He had a hundred things to do, most of them stacked in his briefcase at the hotel.

"I'll be right back. Want a pickle?"

"A pickle?" Alex grimaced in answer and positioned himself under the awning. With a silent growl of annoyance, he looked down at his sneakers, smudged with dirt. Jamming his hands into the pockets of his windbreaker, he squinted up at the sky, expecting a downpour any minute. They should have taken his rental car.

Cooing to Billy, Carly stepped outside with a pickle in her hand. She was a step from Alex when he swung those deep-set green eyes on her. Her steps faltered as excitement unexpectedly fluttered inside her. It was nonsense, of course. Sure, he had the looks to unsettle a feminine heart, but she hardly knew him, wasn't even sure she liked him. To mask her own uneasiness, she plunged into conversation, "What do you do in California?"

Even before she'd spoken, her fragrance had curled around him. "I'm chief executive of operations at Webb Electronics Corporation."

Concentrating on each bite of the pickle helped. Carly stifled a low whistle in response to his words. The title sounded impressive. She wasn't the least bit amazed to learn he was a chief of something. "So you keep everything running smoothly?"

"That's simplifying it, but yes, that's what I do." Alex watched her sink her teeth into the pickle. The corners of her mouth lifted into a smile.

"I love these." Juice on her finger, she offered it to Billy. His nose wrinkled as the tart taste touched his tongue, then he smacked his lips. "Good, huh? You have to wait a while before you get to enjoy these." She took off again, this time walking at a clipped pace.

"Sure you don't want a bite?" she asked, holding out the half-eaten pickle to Alex.

"I'll pass."

Carly thought he did a lot of that in life.

Alex ended his study of the dirt splattering his sneakers in time to sidestep a street barricade.

"Hi, Louie," Carly called out to one of the men excavating. "Working overtime?"

Only his head and shoulders sticking out of the manhole, the man nudged back the brim of his hard hat. "Need the money or I wouldn't be out here in the rain." In his early fifties, he grinned at her with fatherly affection.

"How was the anniversary?" she asked, walking backward to keep talking to him.

Louie's round, unshaven face widened with a deeper grin. "She liked the restaurant."

"Terrific."

"She thought she'd died and gone to heaven with Mel Gibson."

Carly laughed with him and turned around, all the while walking.

Alex matched her stride and caught a whiff of the same fragile scent that had whispered over him yesterday. "Do you talk to everyone?"

"Don't you?" His serious frown told her that she'd wasted breath asking such a question. "What do you do for fun?"

"Stay dry." Alex still couldn't believe he was walking in the rain.

Carly laughed instinctively, saw his glare and cut it short. "That wasn't a joke, was it?"

"No, it wasn't."

She nearly groaned. Clearly, he didn't allow frivolity in his life. Perhaps he would bring a woman flowers and certainly he would offer words to charm her, but their relationship would probably be short on levity. "I'm sorry. I didn't know you didn't like the rain so much."

"I like the rain," Alex snapped because she'd made him sound almost strange for his disagreeableness. If anyone was strange, it was her. "I like watching it rain while I'm sitting in my office."

"But you don't like walking in it?"

Alex shook his head, not in response to her question but to the dumbness of their conversation.

"Well, then, it's good we're almost there."

Alex chanced a look into a restaurant they passed. A dive, it reminded him of a hangout from his youth with its red vinyl booths, black-and-white checkered tile floor and the strong smell of onions. "Where is—"

Carly made a sharp left turn toward a sidewalk vendor. "Hi, Sammy. This is Alex." She smiled over her shoulder at Alex. "Sammy makes the best hot dogs in the city."

Hot dogs! They'd slopped through rain for two blocks for ballpark fare?

"My treat," she announced. "Want everything on yours?"

He should have insisted on knowing their destination. He believed in well-planned actions, on clearly defined intentions, but on the muggy air, her fragrance had drifted over him, taunting his senses. It had muddled his usual logical thought processes.

"Alex?" She peered at him over the top of the wrapped hot dog aimed at her mouth.

Protesting seemed futile. The man with the grizzled hair held a tissue-wrapped bun in his palm and stared expectantly at him. "Everything," Alex answered, sensing she would badger him about why he didn't like onions on his hot dogs if he refused them.

For the past twelve years, Alex had mapped out his life. He'd fought his way through college, doing odd jobs that had ranged from exterminating insects to trimming palm trees. And he'd spent one whole summer at nineteen as the onion slicer at a dive similar to the one they'd passed. He thought he'd left it all behind him. And here he was, eating the kind of food he'd once promised himself he'd never eat again.

Carly couldn't ignore his disdainful expression as she handed him the hot dog. "Hot dogs aren't your style?" she asked when they were out of Sammy's hearing.

Her question amused Alex. Two decades ago, he'd doubted he would ever dine on anything but hot dogs or macaroni and cheese. "Not since I was ten."

The man was a snob, Carly decided. When he'd suggested the move to California, she'd hoped for friendship, but failing that, she was willing to settle for civility. Was that possible? she wondered. "This isn't going to work, is it?"

Alex had had similar thoughts, most of which he'd discarded as quickly as they'd formed. "It will." It had to. Earlier, he'd abruptly become aware of his lack of expertise in handling a baby. Warbling his displeasure, Billy had fussed as if nothing was right in the world. The moment Carly had cooed at him in a soft lilting tone, peace had reigned again. Not once had she looked ruffled. He couldn't have said the same for himself.

With his silence, it occurred to Carly that she wasn't being too bright. She had only the barest knowledge about a man she'd agreed to move miles away with, live with. "Tell me about yourself? Harvard graduate?"

Now Alex did smile. "Stanford." He'd worked up the ladder, just as he'd grown up, the hard way. A college scholarship had helped, and a little sacrifice had been worth everything, even trading his youth for success.

Surprised by his answer, Carly wondered if she'd jumped to the wrong conclusions. She'd seen the impeccable suit, had learned about the powerful job he held and had believed he'd been handed everything. But there was a look in his eyes that declared nothing had been so simple. Veiled below his smooth polished surface, he presented an impression of toughness, of the kind of struggle so intense that only someone who's a fighter can beat.

The silence continued while they ate, he with more gusto than she'd expected. "It's good, isn't it?"

"It's okay." Mustard and relish oozed onto Alex's fingers. The mess annoyed him. The rain irritated him. And the sunny woman beside him baffled him. With difficulty, he maneuvered the half-eaten hot dog to his other hand. Gripping it, he wiped a napkin across the stickiness coating his fingers. Unlike him, she appeared unconcerned with anything but savoring the taste. "It would seem we have nothing in common," he murmured.

Carly agreed. While she liked men who could discuss something other than how much their biceps measured, she usually shied away from serious men. She'd known another one like him, one who'd nearly smothered her with his rules of propriety. But too much was at stake for her to let their differences stop her now. "It might seem that way," she said, dabbing her mouth with a napkin.

Alex sent her a questioning look. "You don't agree?"

Carly heard skepticism in his tone. What would she do if he changed his mind about their agreement? "I'm sure there are some things..." Her voice trailed off as he shook his head.

Alex never backed down from making his point. "I like Mozart. Fine restaurants. You listen to music that sounds like someone running their nails down a chalkboard." He drilled a look at the hot dog she was biting into. "And you eat like a ten-year-old. Pure junk."

"I've thought about that," Carly said with an unexpected thoughtful look. If given a choice, she would have stayed clear of him. She didn't need a stiff, reserved, humorless person in her life. She'd lived with a family like that, had nearly welcomed a man like that into her life. But for Billy, she would do anything. "I've decided that we'll bring a nice balance to Billy."

"Or make him schizophrenic."

Carly cracked a smile. Deeply buried within him, he might possess a sense of humor. "Do you take showers?"

A flicker of amusement crossed his face. "Yes. Are you trying to find out if I bathe regularly?"

She'd already assumed that. The clean male scent of him had bothered her more than once since he'd first stepped into her apartment. "I take showers, too."

Now, Alex understood. She was trying to find common denominators.

"When I take baths, I always feel as if I'm defeating the purpose by sitting in dirty bathwater."

Alex couldn't help it; he laughed.

The rare sound cloaked Carly with a warm sensation. He had a nice laugh, a great smile. She watched it spread to his eyes. The challenge gone from them, they seemed warmer, gentle and even more unsettling.

"I know you're trying to prove—"

Annoyed with herself, she shrugged. "I am proving common ground. We have more in common than some people. In fact, what we share is more important than any differences between us."

"And what is that?"

Her voice softened. "We both care for Billy. That's all that really matters."

Was it? Alex wondered, unable to stop staring at her. He'd never seen any woman look quite so good rain-soaked. At the unexpected heat skittering through him, he relied on logic once more to explain away that feeling. It was natural that an attraction existed. She was different from the women he was accustomed to. In her unusual way, she possessed a quiet sexuality, the kind that hit a man suddenly because she'd tipped her head a certain way or directed that sunshiny smile at him. It made sense that he'd noticed so much. He'd spent more hours with her in the past day than he had with any woman in years.

He'd had to. He needed to know what made her tick, because whether he liked it or not, she would be a part of his life now.

They reached the apartment building before a downpour began. Lost in thoughts of her own, a moment passed before Carly noticed the moving van at the curb.

"Fourth floor," Alex told the two burly-looking men who emerged from the van. "I contacted the moving company yesterday," he informed Carly.

Nerves fluttered in the pit of her stomach. She liked to make her own decisions, had given up all security to do that. "And what about my car?" she asked while dealing with annoyance.

In Alex's mind, debating anything while standing in the rain bordered on stupid. Snagging her arm, he propelled her up the steps. "I'll have it driven to California."

Feeling ornery and stubborn because of his take-charge manner, Carly chose a way to take back control. "Well," she said as they entered her apartment, "some of these cartons that contain Billy's things have to go with us on the plane."

Alex saw no harm in a concession or two. "Okay, a few." Her expression was pensive, gone was the flash of annoyance that had darkened the color of her eyes to a deep blue minutes ago.

"And my potter's wheel."

Alex thought of arguing, then changed his mind. Seconds ago, he'd touched her for no reason except that he'd wanted to. "How much more is there to pack?"

"Only a little more," she assured him.

Chapter Five

Carly was the queen of understatement, Alex decided. Three hours later, they were still packing.

She rolled aching shoulders. She knew he was staring at her. Intense, his gaze challenged every feminine instinct within her. She didn't like that one bit. "I'm going to take Billy to Miriam's and then go to the Top Hat."

With her announcement, she avoided his eyes, and almost nervously, she tucked a strand of hair behind her ear. For some reason, Alex felt a tinge of pleasure that she wasn't as indifferent to him as she pretended. "I thought you already gave your notice."

No matter what he made her feel, Carly knew she would never have a meeting of the minds with someone who didn't understand friendship. "And now I need to say goodbye to my friends," she said, not bothering to

mask her exasperation. "I'll take Billy to Miriam's."
She paused, then issued a challenge. "Unless you want
to stay with him."

Uncertainty flashed in his eyes.

Carly had expected pure panic. While he might want
his son, she knew he didn't know the first thing about
taking care of a baby. When he shook his head, smugly
she hurried down the steps to Miriam's. With Billy in
her arms, Carly rushed an explanation to her that was
only partly the truth.

What she really needed was some breathing space
from Alex. Too often, their hands had brushed when
they'd reached for the same thing. More than once, her
apartment had seemed smaller with him moving around
in it. With every look, with the briefest touch, he'd
made her too aware of a man-woman tug.

She wanted distance, wanted… Carly's steps faltered as she spotted him lounging against the banister
at the foot of the steps. "Where are you going?"

Alex zipped up his windbreaker. "With you."

"You don't have to."

The confusion in her eyes parted lips that looked invitingly soft. That he'd surprised her pleased Alex. But
he felt more, astonishing himself. If she looked at him
like that too often, he could burn for her. "It's late. You
shouldn't walk alone."

"I always walk alone at night."

"I'm around. You don't have to."

The rain plopped steadily. Soaked, Carly preceded
Alex into the Top Hat. Shaking away water dripping
from his jacket, he stalled at the doorway. It would have
served her right if he'd let her come alone. Then only

one of them would look like a drenched idiot. But how could he have? He knew how dangerous the streets had become and didn't want her to jeopardize her safety.

As she weaved a quick path around tables to the bar, a frizzy-haired redhead yelled and ran to her. Tears streaming down her face, she clutched Carly in a bear hug. "Oh, I'm going to miss you so much."

"Renee, I'll call you all the time," Carly promised. She'd tried to prepare for this moment, cognizant it would be the hardest.

"At least once a week," Renee insisted.

"Promise."

It took effort, but Carly got out of the Top Hat without crying.

Alex remained quiet. Vulnerability clouded her eyes despite her attempt at a smile. While he prided himself on being able to deal with most situations, he didn't have a clue how to handle a weepy female.

"That was harder than I expected." She raised her head to see restaurant customers stepping from a limousine.

A tall, gray-haired man's head swiveled in her direction. "Carly. It's nice to see you. Doing okay?"

On a sniff, she rushed a smile. "Just fine, Mayor."

Alex darted a look at the man then at her. Did she know everyone in the whole damn city? "How do you know the mayor so well?"

Carly stepped off the curb with him. "I slept in his office."

"You what?"

She laughed and breezed away. He was such an easy target to shock.

Alex caught her arm, halting her. "Are you going to explain?"

She couldn't stop herself from baiting him. "Are you worried your son's been living with a loose woman?" Eyes that had unnerved her from the beginning locked in a potent stare with hers. Though he'd moved only a fraction closer, his long study made her throat dry. "I marched with protesters, then camped out in his office," Carly managed to say in a voice that sounded nervous even to her own ears.

"What were you trying to change?" Alex asked, but he was more interested in the way the sheen of moisture had darkened her hair than in her answer. He reached over to touch the blond tendrils.

"They weren't allowing the posting of garage sale signs." As he fingered damp strands at her cheek, he seemed to draw nearer. Carly felt the heat of him, and a nervous flutter in her midsection.

"You must have made quite an impact, for him to remember you."

A fierce tug tempted her to sway closer. She resisted, pulling free of the strong hand on her wrist. "I also campaigned for him for reelection."

It took a moment for Alex to make his legs move. He was out of his mind, he decided. He'd been on the verge of kissing her, a woman he not only didn't know but also didn't understand.

Carly reached her apartment first and disappeared into the bedroom to take several of those deep breaths that therapists claimed were guaranteed to relax a person. Carrying an armful of shoes into the living room a short while later, she saw he was busy taping a carton, treating the previous moment as if it had never happened.

Alex couldn't stop thinking about what she'd told him. He would never have expected her to be politically involved. He'd thought her more whimsical, more carefree. Repeatedly, she baffled the hell out of him. How would she fit into his life? The unknown always made him edgy.

As he glanced around the room for other unsealed cartons, his gaze fixed on a chipped secondhand chair. "You don't make a habit of having yard sales, do you?" At her silence, he looked back at her. Was she baiting him again? He hoped so as he considered the posh neighborhood he was moving her to, and the inevitable gasps such an event would draw from a few of his neighbors.

Carly nearly said yes to watch that look of disbelief flutter across his face once more. "No, but I love going to them. There's all that wonderful stuff. And everything's so cheap." The less interaction, the better, she reminded herself and thought of a guaranteed way to put them at odds again. "Wait, I'll show you," she said, flinging open the doors of a cabinet she hadn't emptied yet.

It overflowed with what looked to Alex like junk. It was junk, he determined almost immediately.

Carly ignored what sounded like a groan. Not responding was better—safer. "See, I got this."

Proudly she held up a broken cuckoo clock. Not the least bit interested in what she considered the find of the century, Alex surveyed the mess still around them. "Why did you buy that?" he asked, not hiding his disapproval.

"Because I like it."

"But it's broken. And it's in a cupboard. If you liked it so much, why didn't you have it fixed?"

"No room to display it." With a fingertip, Carly touched the huge chip on the side of the clock then held up a Bavarian beer stein. "I bought this, too. But then I had to get this."

For the life of him, Alex couldn't imagine why. Chipped, the two-inch-high statue was a poor imitation of a Hummel.

With some satisfaction, she saw a tinge of disapproval in his eyes before she reentered the bedroom. Whatever had nearly happened outside the Top Hat would have been a mistake. Keeping distance between them made more sense. Carly lugged the folded swing set from the bedroom for him to carry downstairs. What they didn't need, she decided, was another complication.

Seeming as eager as she was to avoid more nearness, Alex said nothing when she stepped out of the bedroom. He picked up the swing set and left to carry it to the car. Restless, Carly hurried down to Miriam's to get Billy. Uncertainty shadowed her. She constantly seesawed about the deal she'd made with Alex. More than once, she'd nearly told him to forget it. Perhaps she should. It might be better to halt everything now.

Then she snuggled Billy in her arms. No, she couldn't risk losing him. And even if she didn't, Alex would; Billy deserved to know his father. He also definitely needed her.

Trouble. She was a damn lot more trouble than Alex had expected. A damn lot more, he thought, growing more exasperated as he stepped back into the apartment.

Lying on the floor, she had Billy propped on her stomach. "Pattycake, Billy. Pattycake, pattycake, baker's—"

"What are you doing?" Alex motioned toward the junk cabinet. "We've got all this packing to do."

"Relax." Smiling, Carly moved Billy's pudgy hands again and sang out the rhyme.

Relax. That word had never been part of Alex's vocabulary. Survival had dominated his life. Then the long uphill climb. Power. From the time he'd been eleven, he'd wanted it.

"If you don't kick back once in a while, Alex, you won't have time to think about all you've accomplished and enjoy it."

She wasn't crazy; she was going to drive *him* crazy. Softly he swore, then eyed the items she'd set by the door—a high chair, a playpen, the folded stroller. How could one little person need so much? "I'll carry the rest of these down."

"Right-o," Carly sang out to him in her best laid-back, not-a-care-in-the-world voice.

Alex curbed a yell at her to get busy that was threateningly close to slipping out. No woman had ever annoyed him so much or bothered him so quickly.

He couldn't say what it was about her that appealed to him. But then logic had nothing to do with the warmth that spread through him when she smiled, or the craving that curled in the pit of his stomach every time he caught her scent.

Irritated with himself, he remained outside longer than he needed to, letting the cool night air drift over him. And he tried to forget the whispering caress of her hot breath when they'd stood so close outside the lounge.

Every instinct he possessed cautioned him to back off. It was sound advice. Only he had a hell of a time following it as he opened the door of her apartment and saw her. She was bent over a carton. As strands of hair fell across her cheek, he dodged an urge to bury his hand in the tousled softness. No matter what his head told him, he wanted to kiss her.

On a soft oath, he pivoted away. Billy was on the floor, gleefully patting a huge orange ball that Carly had set between his legs. Feeling at odds with himself, Alex looked for something to gentle his mood. As Billy rubbed a fist at his eyes, Alex placed his hands under his son's arms and picked him up. Yawning, his head on Alex's shoulder, Billy trustingly curled one little hand against the **side** of Alex's neck. Something unidentifiable swept over him. Alex couldn't name it. He only knew he felt more at peace.

The doubts Carly harbored about her arrangement with Alex slithered away in that one instant with the token of affection between father and son. No matter how difficult the situation was for her, she would muddle through—for Billy's sake. She and Alex would make this work. For one little boy, they had to succeed.

Half an hour later, Alex packed some more of what she'd deemed a "necessity" into the rental car. An eternity passed before he deposited her potter's wheel in the back seat. She couldn't have much more left up there. The apartment wasn't bigger than his bedroom at home.

Muscles Alex hadn't used in a while ached as he dragged himself up the three flights of steps again. When he'd left the last time, she'd been packing the diaper bag.

Steps from the door, he heard voices, laughter, music. People crowded her small apartment. The lilting sound of a flute drifted from a corner. The guy playing it resembled a throwback to the sixties. A woman with reddish purple hair, who had probably hit the half-century mark twenty years ago, danced with a man dressed in Gypsy garb.

Alex inched his way through the people blocking his path from the door. What the hell was going on now? The cake on the table clarified everything. Written across it was: *Good luck, Carly. We'll miss you.*

"You'll take good care of her, won't you?" a woman asked, touching Alex's arm.

Alex had briefly met Miriam earlier, had seen the sadness in her eyes when Carly had announced her plans. He offered the woman a grin. "Promise," he assured her to ease her mind. Until Miriam's question, Alex had considered only the upheaval Carly would cause in his life. But what about hers? She was giving up a lot. More than once during the next hour he viewed the genuine warmth so many people had for her.

Carly dismissed any hope of staying dry-eyed as the goodbyes began. The final one sent tears streaming down her cheeks. With a promise to keep in touch, she hugged Miriam hard, then closed the door. "That was wonderful. They're all so nice," she said, turning and facing Alex. "I hate losing them."

How did any man resist a woman who looked so needy, so damn vulnerable? Alex wondered. Her eyes brighter, her cheeks a touch flushed, her face glowed from happiness and tears. Whether to comfort or reassure, he wasn't sure, but he placed a hand on her shoulder and drew her close. Strands as soft as silk brushed his fingers. How slim she was amazed him because she exhibited such toughness. With her proud face raised to him, and her eyes misty with tears, he started to lower his head, to seek the mouth that looked so inviting to him.

The mental lapse lasted only a second. As if he'd been jabbed in the back, he straightened and released her. To do anything else would have been one gigantic mistake that would mess up everything. "I'll be back," he murmured and headed for the door. "I need to check on the company plane." What he really needed was time to clear his head.

Shaken, Carly slouched down on a sofa cushion. What she needed was quiet time to sort through her own confused feelings. Why was there such a physical attraction to a man who offered everything she'd escaped from? When she'd agreed to the arrangement, she'd hoped for friendship eventually between them. But this, whatever it was that kept happening, promised big problems.

The same thought returned when Carly settled on the plane seat beside Alex several hours later. She'd already noticed the tinge of red in his dark hair when he'd stood in the sunlight before they'd boarded the plane. She'd been too aware of his eyes on her, their directness and their wariness. He was hardly her type. Not having goals was a mortal sin to people like him and her aunt. She could have told Alex that she didn't flutter through life, that in her own way and at her own pace, she'd strived for artistic achievements. She'd always believed that without ambition, dreams wither away. She could have explained all that, but why should she have to? Hadn't she fled all that need for constant explanation years ago?

As Billy rested his head against her breast, Carly angled a stare out the window at fluffy white clouds and moved again on the lumpy seat for what seemed the umpteenth time to find a comfortable spot. Solemn and silent, Alex had been engrossed in paperwork from the briefcase he'd opened on his lap even before takeoff.

So be it, Carly decided.

"Have you ever considered meditating?" Alex asked, more annoyed with himself than her because no amount of concentration eased his awareness of her.

Carly considered his question. She would have tagged Alex as more of a doer than a contemplator. "Do you meditate?"

Alex couldn't imagine wasting time doing that. "No, but some people find it calming."

Now she understood. "You think I need to calm down?"

"You're fidgety."

Better than being comatose, she mused.

With unseeing eyes, Alex gazed again at typewritten lines on the report before him. During previous trips on the company plane, the drone of the engine usually went unnoticed, the clouds outside the window unappreciated and the slight turbulence ignored. This trip began differently. He was aware of everything. Everything. All because of her.

For what it was worth, he managed to read one page of the report before his mind strayed again. Even her laughter intruded. It hung in the air like a ringing in his ears as she cooed at his son and bobbed the dumb-looking purple giraffe in the air. And now she was singing. A musical whispery sound filled Alex's mind while she sang a ridiculous verse about an itsy-bitsy spider.

Fog rolled in from the ocean. San Francisco was glass-and-steel skyscrapers and Victorian houses. Oddly, Carly felt a tinge of homesickness for the city she'd left willingly years ago.

During the drive into the southern Bay Area, she absorbed the sight of lush, manicured grounds and prestigious homes like a tourist. She thought about her family—her aunt and dear cousin Christian, the perfect son.

"This is home to you, isn't it?" Alex squinted against the sunlight glaring against the car window and casting her face in shadow.

Never home, Carly reflected, bending forward and switching on the stereo. She'd left her aunt's home and had never looked back. "Born and raised here," she said lightly. Since Alex didn't object, she fiddled with the dial to tune in a song made famous by the Eagles.

"Why did you leave?"

Carly gave an easy answer, one he would expect from her. "I wanted to see more." As the mellow sounds filled the car, she focused on the scenery once more. All the while, lyrics about letting love in before it's too late hummed in her head.

Over the rim of his mirrored sunglasses, Alex glanced at her. "Did you say something?"

Had she? She shook her head. Imagination again. Nothing more.

Chapter Six

As Alex turned the car onto a circular driveway lined with a plethora of flowers, nothing prepared Carly for the imposing brick English Tudor Alex called home.

She felt a bit like Alice in Wonderland as she moved mechanically from the car. Carrying Billy in his carrier seat, she preceded Alex into the house. Her gaze floated over the crystal chandelier, the curving staircase. At Alex's urging, she ambled through the bay-windowed living room with its marble fireplace, the elegant formal dining room, the paneled library with built-in bookcases, the large sun room with its hardwood floors and panoramic windows.

She couldn't imagine a child's smeary fingerprints on the highly glossed baby grand piano or on the silver coffee server that sat regally on a sideboard. Wandering, she detected an interior decorator's professional touches, from the placement of paintings on the wall to the perfect positioning of the onyx chess set and exotic ashtray on the coffee table. Exquisite came to mind. Definitely an executive's domain. But where would Billy fit in? And what about her?

"Guess you do pretty well," she said, dropping Billy's diaper bag to the floor.

Standing in the living room's arched doorway, Alex riffled through his mail. "Acceptable."

Carly stifled a snort. Billy had a rich daddy. "It's lovely," she murmured.

Alex dropped the envelopes onto a nearby table and gazed at her. Dressed in casual cream-colored slacks and a pullover top in soft beige, she looked classy, she almost looked as if she belonged in a house like this. "Let me show you the upstairs."

She didn't belong here was Carly's first thought when she stood in the doorway of the room he'd indicated was hers. Years ago when she'd left her aunt's home, she'd taken herself out of this world. It seemed insane to be back in it.

At her unnatural silence, Alex wanted to offer some kind of assurance to ease away the frown knitting her eyebrows. "If you don't care for it—"

Carly swung a disbelieving look at him. What woman wouldn't love the four-poster bed, the mahogany dressing table or the finely crafted quilt rack and the heirloom coverlet draped over it? Regal and romantic, the room was decorated in the William and Mary period of elegance. "This is perfect." And that bothered her. Carly had shied away from anything perfect since she was nine years old as, clinging to her brother's hand, she'd stood in the living room of her aunt's house. Before she'd turned fifteen, Carly had quietly referred to it as the mausoleum. "Where will Billy be?"

Ending his fascination with her mouth, Alex stepped back, but he knew something intangible was magnetizing him to a woman who countered everything he believed in. "In here," he said, opening a connecting door. "That's why I chose this room for you."

If she'd known he'd offered all this, Carly doubted she would have agreed. What he'd worked so hard for, she'd shunned. Circling Billy's room, she motioned toward the French door that led onto a balcony. "I love that," she said with genuine pleasure as she envisioned enjoying a sunrise with Billy from that terrace.

Long ago, Alex had stopped caring about anyone's opinions except his own, but he realized he'd been waiting for a token of approval from her. "I'll have this furniture moved and stored today, so his crib can be brought in."

Carly had to ask. "And where will you be?"

Alex pointed to a door on the opposite wall of the nursery. "We both can check on him."

Nibbling her top lip, Carly shifted a sleeping Billy to her other shoulder. "Cozy."

The small hint of nerves amused Alex. "There's a lock on your door."

Carly whipped around. He wasn't smiling, but she would swear she'd heard laughter in his voice. Impossible. Alex was too serious for teasing humor. Wasn't he?

"You can change anything. I'll leave the decorating of the nursery to you."

His words pleased Carly, but even as her mind spun with ideas, it was his stare that warmed her. She saw gentleness in his eyes again, and suddenly her heart was pounding too fast. Confused, she swung away to see a plump, gray-haired woman in the doorway.

"Where's this suitcase belong?" the woman asked and marched in.

"It's my suitcase." Eager to make a friend, Carly closed the distance to her. "I'm Carly."

Though the woman had a face that spoke of a hard life and a lot of living, it softened when she looked at Billy asleep against Carly's breast. "I'm Dora. He's a cutie."

Carly smoothed down Billy's dark hair. "Yes, he is."

"Alex said you came because you love the boy," Dora said with a casualness that denoted a friendship more than an employer-employee relationship with Alex. "That's a fine reason."

Alex had thought so, too. But he hadn't considered other problems, not really. Like one slim blonde making him feel as physically charged as he'd been at seventeen. Mumbling to himself, he left the room and headed for the stairs.

"It all sounds crazy to me," Dora said, trailing him.

Alex shrugged at her unasked-for opinion and descended the staircase with her. "It'll work."

She smirked in a way that indicated he hadn't convinced her. "Well, here are your messages. All from Diana Keenan."

Alex took the slips of paper from her. "I'll call her later."

"I don't think so." With her thumb, Dora gestured to the white Corvette pulling into the driveway.

Carly opened the terrace doors in the nursery and stilled as murmured voices drifted up to her. Tall and leggy, a polished-looking woman had emerged from a white Corvette. In heels, she stood almost eye-to-eye with Alex. Hair as dark as his shimmered beneath the sunlight when she stepped intimately close and kissed him. Oddly, Carly hadn't considered that there might be a woman waiting for his return. How foolish of her. A man his age with so much to offer would never remain unattached. She noted that the woman's smile was fading and her voice was raising in anger. Carly turned away. Whatever was happening outside between them wasn't her business.

While Billy napped in his carrier seat, she wandered downstairs and through the doors to the flower garden. A lush, landscaped lawn sloped down a hill to a small pond. The quietness would take some getting used to. She'd become accustomed to the sound of neighbors' voices and blaring stereos. She'd become acclimatized to a simpler life-style—by choice.

For a long moment, Alex watched Diana race her car down the driveway. He hadn't thought about her reaction to the change in his life. Hell, he was still adjusting to it himself.

He turned and spotted Carly wandering in the garden. Blond hair that reminded him of wheat swayed beneath the sunlight. With his approach, she smiled, and a hint of a dimple cut into her cheek. He hadn't noticed it before. He hadn't noticed the faint spray of freckles on her nose, either.

"This is lovely," Carly said honestly about the garden of colorful blooms and the trees surrounding the pond.

"I'm glad you like it." A gentle summer breeze whirled around them, tugging at her blouse, molding it to her breasts. Alex looked away. "I had company a few minutes ago."

Carly had learned when to keep her mouth shut. Now seemed like a perfect time.

As she strolled back to the house with him, Alex decided to tell her what gossips would relay eventually. "Her name is Diana Keenan. I've been seeing her for over a year. She knew why I had gone out of town, but I suppose she didn't expect me to find my son. There were times I had my doubts, too. It seems she isn't happy to learn about my instant fatherhood."

That snagged Carly's full attention. Was he going to tell her Billy was hers again?

"She said that children aren't something she wants to include in her life. She's a busy woman." He said it matter-of-factly, conveying the tone she'd used. "So she suggested I let you take the baby back to Colorado with you since you're so devoted to him."

Quit telling me what she *said. What did* you *say?*

Her eyes, dark and large and questioning, pinned him. "I told her I couldn't do that. And she politely told me to go to hell."

Carly frowned. "I'm sorry." She was a mush. Too much of one, Carly knew. While he'd talked, she'd been filled with the inevitable softness that surfaced whenever someone shared their trouble with her. "Was she— are you hurting?"

Amused at the notion, Alex laughed. "Hardly. But I did enjoy her company." He wasn't lying. Diana had provided him with a necessary companion, but he'd never expected to make a lifetime commitment to her. And he wasn't surprised about the split with her. His parents had taught him well. Relationships unraveled easily beneath stress.

"I have to go to the office for a little while," he said. Alex reached around her to open the back door. "But I'll see that the crib is brought up first." Her fragrance teased him again. This time, he drifted with it, turning his head and bringing his mouth a hairbreadth from hers. He felt the jolt to his system as desire came on a rush. "Oh, hell. We have to get this out of the way." Without thinking more about his actions, Alex slid his hand to the curve of her waist.

Carly drew a quick shaky breath. She could feel the heat of him, smell the life in him. "This?"

"This," Alex said, never taking his eyes off her lips. He swore at himself a second before his mouth closed over hers. Somewhere deep in his mind, during every aggravating moment with her, he'd been wondering about her taste. He knew now. It was sweet, so sweet that it was almost addictive. He twisted his lips against hers, taking deeply, filling himself.

He felt something foreign overwhelming him—an impatience for more. Never had one kiss aroused him so quickly. No, it wasn't only the kiss. It was the restless emotion she was awakening in him that he was unprepared for. He wanted to hear her whisper his name in that smoky voice. He wanted to touch her. It amazed him how badly he wanted to put his hands on her.

Desire he understood, but not the recklessness leading him. For this moment, he couldn't think about an hour from now much less the next day or the following weeks. A slow-moving ache gnawed at him. Driven by a wildness that seemed alien, he drew her tighter to feel every soft contour.

Carly heard her moan. Of protest or pleasure? She wasn't sure. With her arms around his neck, she strained against him. The kiss was far from what she'd expected from him. Firm, hard lips captured her mouth in a long, lingering manner that insisted on response. She tasted experience. Persuasion. She felt as if she were drowning beneath sensation.

A message of seduction, promised passion and urgency whispered in the air around them. It was all so insane. She shouldn't be aching. She shouldn't be answering him. She shouldn't want more.

Even as he drew back, as she opened her eyes, the struggle within herself went on. Her bones felt soft, her legs unsteady. It hadn't been just a kiss. She'd been wrapped up in him even before the kiss—warmed by a smile, excited by his closeness, flushed with heat from something as simple as a look. As she pressed a hand to his chest to force distance between them, his eyes locked with hers. Though he no longer touched her, he was pulling her nearer. Breathless, she resisted. "That was pleasant, but—"

"Pleasant?" Alex cut in. Her taste still lingering on his lips, he vividly recalled her sighs. No way was he the only one who'd felt the earth move.

"Alex, it would be crazy to let this get out of hand." He seemed to inch closer again. "It's not reasonable," she said on a rush.

Slowly he smiled. At some moment, they'd slipped into each other's shoes. With her scent luring him and the warmth of her lips still a part of him, he didn't give a damn about what was reasonable.

Carly wanted to be firm. Instead, she felt weak, laboring for each breath as he lightly toyed with a strand of her hair. "You said this was a business deal. Strictly business."

The reminder annoyed him because he suddenly wanted to take back those words. But he considered himself an honorable man, one who was good for his word. "Strictly business," he echoed and let her step forward, away from him.

Strictly business. Alex rarely recanted, but doubts surfaced that he would maintain such a relationship with her.

Like polite strangers, they dealt with the unpacking. While Billy snoozed in his carrier seat, they hauled up Carly's "must have" cartons. From one of them, she removed a crib sheet and comforter. Behind her, Alex and a man he'd introduced as the gardener maneuvered Billy's crib into the room.

Billy's stirring caught her attention, and she watched him as he looked around, his eyes darting. At everything new or for something familiar? Carly wondered and picked him up. She wished she felt more comfortable in the huge home. She assumed that in time she would, but at the moment, all that Alex offered surged her with panic, from the promise of more in his kiss to his home so like another stately house in her memory. There, the coldness had pervaded its rooms even on the warmest days. "It won't be like that for you," she murmured, hugging Billy tighter, "I promise."

But what about Alex? She couldn't forget that kiss or the heat of his mouth. Amazingly, she couldn't think of one man in her life who'd ever launched so much reaction with just one kiss. But was his kiss really special? If any man had kissed her so gently, so thoroughly, wouldn't she have felt the same way? She would be a fool to get carried away by romantic notions. Except for that knock-your-socks-off kiss, she and Alex were hardly compatible. Strictly business, he'd said, hadn't he? If she was wise, she would forget the kiss, the sparks, the way her body had melted in his arms.

Setting Billy in his crib, she watched his eyes open wide, searching. As he whimpered, Carly picked him up and zigzagged a path around cartons. "I don't know where it is," she said while she scanned the room for the purple giraffe.

For the next half hour, Alex closeted himself in his study. He'd decided that everything with Carly was sexual. So nothing more would happen. He would make sure of that.

With the silence around him, a sense of normalcy drifted over him, the first time in days since he'd felt it. The house was merely a symbol of how hard he'd worked to leave his beginnings behind him. What he'd missed most was the tranquillity, the sense of order, the solitude and peaceful quietness. He was a loner. He preferred answering only to himself, taking his own advice—depending on no one else. He always had. Now wasn't the time to forget any of that.

He climbed the steps to check on Billy before he left for the office. Discarded cartons were heaped in the center of the room and stacks of clothing concealed the surfaces of dressers. Carly's organizational skills bordered on disastrous.

With care, Alex weaved his way around the toys sprawled everywhere. A foot from the crib, he saw Carly kneeling on the floor beside one carton. Rocking Billy, she looked anguished. "What's wrong?"

Eyes filled with worry turned up to him. "His purple giraffe isn't here," she whispered.

Alex couldn't comprehend her catastrophic expression over a stuffed animal, but he asked what he considered a logical question, "Did you pack it?"

"I took it with us on the airplane," she said while gently patting Billy's back.

Alex dropped to his haunches near her and tipped his head to see his son. His eyes closed, his hands fisted, Billy's chest rose and fell steadily with the peace of slumber. "I wouldn't worry. He's going to sleep."

"I know, but he already looked for it. I could tell," she said in a low voice. "And when he awakens, he'll look for it again."

"I doubt he'll be as upset as you are." Alex nearly touched her. "Do you want me to help you look?"

If he'd understood her concern, she would have welcomed his offer, but he didn't comprehend that something that seemed trivial to him was security to Billy. "I'll keep looking," she answered softly.

For the moment, Alex accepted her refusal. "Don't worry," he said while pushing to a stand.

Alone, she worried about more than Billy. Every time Alex's eyes met hers, an undercurrent of tension rippled through the air. It was important she control her emotions. He could hurt her, she reminded herself. She'd learned the lesson early in life. When she'd reached out for love with a man like him, she'd been hurt. She wouldn't be again. She wouldn't forget they weren't suitable for each other.

Alex had thought woman trouble was his biggest problem.

Arriving at the office, he learned he was wrong.

The board of directors greeted his announcement about Billy with two expressions—gaping surprise and scowls.

Only Hoagan, the retiring CEO, looked amused. "She's the baby's nanny then?" Hoagan asked.

Alex met the man's curious gaze. "She's his adoptive aunt. Because of her attachment to my son, maintaining an amiable relationship with her was necessary."

Nob Hill's grande dame, Leone Pipperton, tipped her head questioningly. "I'm not quite certain I understand. Is she living with you?"

"She's in my home, and she'll care for my son."

Leone cocked a thin, gray eyebrow. "I assume you had a background check on this Carly Mitchell."

Background. It meant nothing to Alex. Unlike most of the people in the room who came from generations of well-established families and old money, he'd climbed the ladder of success from neither.

"There's no need," Bennett Doleman said, garnering everyone's attention. "Her full name is Carly Rochelle Criswell Mitchell." The chairman of the board went on, "I know her personally. She and my youngest daughter played in the school orchestra at Bainworth Boarding School. Her mother was Lionel Criswell's daughter." Doleman smiled. "If I recall correctly, Carly played the harp—no, the flute."

"Criswell?" Alex repeated, still registering what attending the private girls' school implied. Money. A pedigree. The woman talked to sewer workers and ate hot dogs from sidewalk vendors. She'd worked her cute little butt off in a lounge. Why hadn't she gone to her family for financial help? Why had she been living with Billy in a cramped fourth-floor apartment?

The questions nagged at Alex. He didn't understand her. No one shunned that kind of background willingly.

Except for the ticking of a grandfather clock, silence surrounded Carly. Though Billy had settled down for her, she anticipated short-lived quiet. In the shower, she fretted some more about the giraffe. She'd set a panda in his crib but doubted that would satisfy him. Tonight, she would sleep in a chair by his crib. If he awakened, he would become frightened by his strange surroundings, especially since his favorite toy was missing.

How much more could go wrong? she wondered, had been wondering ever since one kiss had curled her toes.

"Alex." The hand of Bennett Doleman clamped on Alex's shoulder, halting his progress from the conference room to his office. "I had wanted to talk to you before the meeting. However, that seemed unnecessary. I saw a positive attitude from all of them regarding you."

Alex gave him a half smile, grateful he had Doleman's endorsement as the company's next CEO. "That's encouraging."

Doleman urged him to resume walking. "While your youth might be a disadvantage, no one can find fault with the changes you've implemented since you've begun handling operations."

Reaching his office door, Alex stopped again. He never believed men in Doleman's position idled away time with inconsequential conversation. With a patience Alex had forced himself to nurture, he waited for Doleman to reveal what he really wanted to say.

"You've kept your personal life spotless, which is important to some of the board members, Leone Pipperton for instance. I know you're aware that the CEO of any company is under a microscope periodically."

Alex sent him a wry smile.

"It seems that Leone is perturbed to learn that you're no longer seeing Diana Keenan."

Nearly smiling, Alex stifled his amazement that such news had traveled like wildfire. "Why is that so bothersome?"

"Always direct. I admire that most about you."

Alex intentionally remained silent.

"Diana was an asset, the right background and schools, the perfect social connections. A very polished young woman."

"I enjoyed her companionship."

"I see."

Alex stifled a laugh. Doleman looked absolutely baffled about how to proceed.

After a moment's hesitation, he nodded understandingly. "Your relationship with her really wasn't our concern. However—" Again, he paused. "Your arrangement with Carly Mitchell might be," he finally said as if he'd given up trying to determine a tactful way to mention it.

"I explained before. It's a practical one. She's my son's adoptive aunt."

"Could she be more?"

Alex narrowed his eyes. "Pardon?"

"For the good of your image, Alex, have you considered a more permanent relationship with her?"

"Such as?"

"Marriage. My boy, marriage would eliminate any negativity about you as our new CEO."

Chapter Seven

Alex made one out-of-the-way stop while weathering rush-hour traffic on the way home that night. The extra time to himself wasn't wasted. He needed it as Doleman's words nagged at him. *Marriage.* The idea was too farfetched. Wasn't it?

Sure, he felt an attraction for Carly. True, she had the right background to please the hierarchy at Webb, but marriage? He'd always believed in setting boundaries in relationships and no promises. Too many people made them with abandon, the same way they uttered words of love. Believing in the staying power of another person, people vowed to love forever. But at the first sign of trouble, they usually split. No, marriage had never entered his mind. Never.

Entering the house, he prepared himself for the mess in the nursery. Instead, surprise swept over him. Cartons had miraculously disappeared. Neat, the room already smelled of baby powder.

Quietly, Alex strolled toward the crib. As he'd forecasted, his son slept, appearing to be unaffected by the missing stuffed toy. He was so innocent-looking. It amazed Alex that everyone started out looking so damn cute, probably even the crotchety Leone Pipperton. Now *there* was a transformation, he mused, smiling and placing the blanket Billy had kicked away back on the child's legs.

From the next room came the sound of rushing water. While the adjustment to having a baby in his life wasn't as difficult as he'd expected, nothing with Carly was going as he'd planned. Absolutely nothing, he realized, standing still as thoughts flooded him of the steam, of the heat, of her offering a shoulder to the water, lifting a slender leg toward the misty warmth.

Alex straightened away from the crib, and on a soft oath, he turned. That's when he saw her in the doorway. Her head bent, she was tying her robe. She ambled forward, seemingly unaware of him, and with each step she took closer to him, all he could think about was the hint of soap and wildflowers, the caressing snugness of her robe at her breasts and hips. While she was still out of his reach, he spoke, "Settled in?"

Startled, Carly jumped. How long had he been there? Her hand to her chest, she drew a stabilizing breath. "I didn't know you were here."

Damp, her hair curled at the tips. It took effort not to bury his hand in the shiny softness. She looked cute. Damn cute.

"I think I know what happened to the giraffe," Carly said in an effort to prevent another one of those meaningful silences between them. "I must have—" Carly cut her words short as she bent over the crib. She touched Billy's cheek. Peaceful, Billy slept, his hand curled around the silly-looking purple giraffe. "Oh, Alex. You found it."

"It was on the plane." In fascination, he followed a droplet trickling down the slender curve of her neck to the collar of her robe. Was the flesh beneath it water-slick? Would his hands glide over the soft skin? Oh, hell, he had a major problem. "We need to talk, Carly."

Still smiling, Carly raised her face to him. "About what...?" Her voice trailed off. Heat. She saw it in his eyes. In a tiny show of nerves, she leaned away from him as she sensed one more touch, or a kiss, and there would be no turning back.

"Not here. I want to take you out." His voice sounded quieter, more intimate. "Someplace nice."

She stared dumbfoundedly at him. "Someplace nice?"

"For dinner. I'll talk to Dora about baby-sitting."

Carly merely nodded.

When Alex had made the suggestion, he hadn't been sure what he'd planned to say to her later. He certainly hadn't expected her to bowl him over. And he'd never have visualized her looking so—what? What word would best describe her?

Wearing a high-necked dress with a slinky length of ivory sleeve and a daring slit that exposed a hint of thigh when she walked, she looked sophisticated. Sexy.

"Is this a favorite place of yours?" Carly asked after they'd been seated at a table.

She turned her head, and the candlelight caught the glow of her hair—and the worry in her eyes. "Too stuffy for you?"

Carly peered over the top of the menu at him. Actually, she liked the restaurant. Appointed with brass and dark wood, it was dimly lit and the soft sounds of a piano played in the background. A romantic ambience of cozy isolated booths allowed for privacy and private conversations. "Do they serve hot dogs?"

He caught her grin of amusement before she looked away. The humor faded so swiftly, Alex wondered if she was suddenly ill. "Are you all right?"

"Fine," Carly answered weakly. But she wasn't as she watched one particular man leaving the restaurant.

Alex followed her stare and zeroed in on a tall Ivy Leaguer in a gray pin-striped suit. He cut his way around tables toward the exit as if he owned the restaurant. A quick first impression declared him a Nob Hill type who would demonstrate perfect manners to those he deemed worthy. All others would receive a nose-in-the-air response. Alex's own beginnings had been too simple for such a transformation to ever happen to him. "Someone you know?"

She'd never really known him, Carly reflected. "Austin Westerly III. Someone from my past."

By the tension tightening her features, Alex didn't believe her casual act. But there was a lot he didn't know about her. Besides the minor fact that she came from old money, there loomed some history with an artist.

As the waiter hovered, taking their orders and pouring their wine, Alex passed time telling humorous Dora stories.

Despite smiles, Carly continued to wrestle nerves about this spur-of-the-moment dinner invitation. "She was really a sergeant in the army?"

Sitting back, Alex smiled at the interested gleam in her eyes. "Why wouldn't you believe that?"

"I do. But in just hours, I've seen how loving and funny she is with Billy. She talks to him like Donald Duck and sings songs from 'Sesame Street' to him and—she's just wonderful with him."

"So are you," Alex said honestly.

The compliment thrilled her more than any she'd ever heard from a man. "I love him, Alex."

"I know you do. That's why we have to discuss something."

Carly dragged in a deep breath.

Alex poked at a piece of prime rib, then set down his fork. Sound logical. List reasons. Focus on the end results. "If we're honest with each other, no one will get hurt."

Carly's frown deepened. Where was this conversation going? She toyed with the thin stem of her water goblet, and silently waited for him to go on while her heart banged so hard it felt as if it would burst through her chest.

"Within weeks, a new CEO will be named at Webb Electronics."

Carly heard a trace of pleasure in his voice. "You?"

"I have a good chance. Better than good," he admitted. "But I need a settled, stable image."

Carly sensed his next words. *You're complicating everything.* She watched him reaching into the breast pocket of his suit coat. Had bringing her to California been calculated to get Billy here, then get rid of her?

Was he about to hand her an airplane ticket for a flight back to Denver? Head down, she smoothed the napkin in her lap. *I'm not leaving Billy,* she vowed determinedly. *He's too precious to me.*

"Carly?"

Her stomach knotted as she prepared herself for his scowl, for the logical-sounding edge in his voice, for the cut-and-dried words of dismissal. Raising her eyes, she stared, but her mind went blank.

On the table between them, glittering under the candlelight, was the most gorgeous diamond engagement ring she'd ever seen. A circle of sparkling diamonds winked, while the one in the center danced with a rainbow of color. She didn't realize she was holding her breath until a sigh escaped her lips.

"For both of us, marriage might eliminate many problems."

Carly couldn't speak. This was the second time he'd knocked the wind from her with one of his ideas.

Alex saw a multitude of emotions in her face and couldn't zero in on any of them. Was it absurd to think she would be willing to take such a step as marriage with him? "It would be a sensible arrangement for both of us," he went on. "I need a mother for my child."

Carly fixed a stare on the ring. How could he offer something so beautiful, and in the next breath propose marriage in such a no-nonsense tone?

"You would permanently have the child you don't want to give up."

Oh, yes, that was important to her.

"Also—"

Carly slanted a look at him.

"You would have a chance to further your career because of my business ties to influential and affluent people."

She couldn't help it; she laughed. "We hardly know each other."

He believed truth was his only ace in the hand. "We'll learn."

Carly raised a halting hand to him. "Wait! Why? Why do you really want to get married?"

"I've been reminded that our living arrangement might be bad for my image."

"The powers that be aren't happy about us living together?"

"Something like that."

Candlelight danced across her face as she shook her head. "That's archaic thinking. Did you explain that I'm Billy's adoptive aunt?"

Alex said the obvious. "You're also young and beautiful."

Carly's eyebrows veed as she felt excitement sweep through her. Men had favored her with compliments before but none of them had done that to her. Determined not to get lost in the fog of pleasure, she rushed questions. "Are all the people who work at Webb married? Don't any of them live with someone?"

"Not people trying to be the CEO of their multimillion-dollar corporation."

Still dealing with her own shock, Carly ran a finger down the stem of her wineglass. "So if you didn't want to be the CEO, they wouldn't care?"

"Probably not."

She tightened her grip on the wineglass, but she didn't drink. What she needed most was a clear head. "You do have a problem, Alex."

"I thought so." His expression grew more serious. "Either I marry you or—"

"I have to leave," Carly finished for him. And then what? The dreaded custody battle? She stared thoughtfully at him. Surely he knew they weren't good for each other. "You might have more problems if you do marry me. You need a suitable woman who would love to play hostess to your colleagues, and your friends and acquaintances." That wasn't her. She dressed in the first thing handy she found in the closet, not some designer's dream. She spent her days playing with clay not volunteering for charities. She preferred junk food not cuisine fit for royalty. "I'm hardly what you need in your life."

The same thought had crossed his mind more than once, but he would never have made this decision if he hadn't thought they could give his son a happy family, if Alex hadn't felt a deepening appeal for her. And there was the old kick in the gut that he had to deal with every time she was too close. That he wanted her made the decision easier. "I'll be honest." He hunched forward, but he didn't touch her. "I never planned to marry." He paused for a moment, then said grimly, "Regardless of their good intentions, people can't or don't keep promises."

Carly wondered who'd taught him that.

"But you and I are already bound to each other by Billy."

Carly clenched her hands. "And what you're suggesting is a business arrangement?"

Alex smiled instinctively. "Not totally. We both know it could be more," he said, reminding her of the kiss. "In time." For the marriage to have any chance of working, they couldn't ignore sex. He gave his head a shake because he couldn't recall ever having such a discussion with a woman. Passion sort of just happened. Noting the frown line marring her forehead, he offered the best assurance possible. "For now, we'll take time to get used to each other." At her silence, Alex gauged the only possible reason for her hesitancy. "There's no one else in your life right now. Is there?"

"No." Foolish or not, she'd been waiting to meet the man she could promise forever to. Austin had taught her to be true to her own feelings above everything. But Alex wasn't pretending love. He'd been speaking logically, listing reasons.

"We could talk about this later," he told her.

Carly felt compelled to say, "There are a lot of reasons why this might not work." They were as different as night and day in their thinking. They would constantly be at odds. "I never wanted someone like you in my life," she admitted.

His eyes narrowed. "Like me?"

"Too perfect."

Alex released a short laugh and touched her hand. "I'd be pleased with that, if I didn't think I'd just been insulted."

Immediately, Carly slid her hand from his. With his touch, her mind was clouding. "This will complicate everything."

Alex thought about Doleman, about Leone Pipperton, about a job he'd strived for, about a son he'd already learned to love. "Everything is more complicated than I expected."

"Then why make it worse?"

Alex doubted the choice was theirs. "I don't think we will be. We're not going into it with illusions that we're a match made in heaven."

The reminder made her frown again. Hardly that. But she'd never imagined agreeing to a marriage because it was convenient.

"I've given you some reasons. But the most important reason is my son needs a mother." Alex waited for her to look up at him. "And you're already that to him."

Masterfully, he'd zeroed in to touch her heart. "He would be mine legally?"

"Of course."

Wasn't that what she wanted most? It hadn't taken her long to realize that a move into Alex's house with Billy might prevent a custody battle, but offered no guarantees. Marriage would. Marriage and certain legalities meant Billy couldn't be taken from her.

"If you say yes, we'll fly to Vegas tonight. But I would understand if you want time to consider—"

"No," she cut in, almost afraid to let herself think long and hard about what she was doing. If Alex felt compelled to marry because of his career, then another woman would inevitably usurp her place in his home. The appearance of Diana Keenan had emphasized how tenuous her own position was in Billy's life. Carly couldn't stand the thought of being separated from Billy. For her, there was only one reason, and only one answer. "I'll marry you," she said softly as thoughts about Billy outweighed all the arguments she might think of later.

A neon-lit oasis, Las Vegas welcomed. Casinos resounded with the noise of coins clinking near the slot machines and the roulette wheel spinning.

It wasn't *the* wedding of the century. It wasn't even the kind of wedding Carly had dreamed about having.

In gaudy fashion, the garish chapel had a cutesy name. A slightly out-of-tune piano player's abbreviated rendition of "Oh, Promise Me" provided a semblance of romance. Carly had yearned for a meadow of flowers, for the feel of the wind on her face, for all the romantic trimmings that love songs promised.

Her fingers tightened on the small bouquet of pink tea roses that Alex had gotten her. Under the bright casino lights, the gold band Alex had slid on her finger shimmered. Within fifteen minutes they'd been married. She thought about the brief ceremony, the form they'd signed, the minister whose Adam's apple had bobbed while he'd unemotionally spieled out the words that had legally bound her to Alex.

Wanting to absorb the sweeter portions of the past moments, she inhaled the scent of the roses. "It was thoughtful of you to buy these."

Alex tucked the paper they'd signed into his pocket. The flowers seemed like so little to him. Despite his no-nonsense manner, he valued the effect of romance. "I'm sorry this wasn't—well, most women want white lace and champagne, don't they?"

Carly could live without that kind of romance. "As you said, we have no illusions about why we got married." What she needed most was a family to love. With a child's open heart, she'd gone to live at her aunt and uncle's. It hadn't taken her long to recognize that they'd done what was expected of them. They'd been charitable.

Love? No, she hadn't found that. Instead, she'd known years of being told she didn't fit in. And, oh, how she'd longed to. She'd heard constant comments about her impulsiveness and her lack of logic, and had yearned to please. Nothing she'd ever done had satisfied them. She'd never been logical enough. She still wasn't, she mused.

Impulsively, she'd plunged into a marriage with Alex. Logic had played no part in her decision. Emotion had led her. She needed Billy, and he needed her.

Carly couldn't keep her nerves at bay. After arriving back at the house, Dora insisted on a celebratory glass of champagne. Alex humored the woman but was honest about why they'd married. Dora scowled and walked away, clucking her tongue.

Alone with Alex, Carly was caught up in her own conflicting emotions. She set the glass of champagne aside and poured coffee, keeping her back to him a moment longer. A funny feeling, as if she were a breath away from being attacked by intestinal flu, somersaulted her stomach every time the diamond on her finger winked at her beneath the light. "Do you want some coffee?"

"Sure." Hours ago, Alex would have avoided finding out what was bothering her. Now, things were different. Now, she was his wife. He raked a hand through his wind-tossed hair. Married. He still couldn't believe it. While he would make sure emotion didn't complicate a situation already unbelievably complex, he couldn't ignore her moment-to-moment feelings. "Is everything all right?"

Carly returned her attention to the coffee steaming in her cup. "This might sound dumb to you, but I realized this is my first act as a wife," she said, turning with a cup for him.

"So what's wrong?"

"I wondered if you were having doubts."

Hundreds. His eyebrows knit. "Are you?"

Too many to count. What did he expect now? He'd said he would give her time. "A few, but I don't have as many expectations as you do."

Alex didn't like the way that made him sound. "I only expect one thing from you." He ran a hand down her arm, wanting the touch of her skin but expecting nothing else.

Carly had braced herself for sensations but wasn't prepared for the heat radiating through her body or the need humming within her.

"And you already do that," Alex said softly, drawing back. "You love my son."

On an unsteady breath, she watched him leave the room. Feelings undefined for him before were now even more confusing.

In her own bedroom, Carly desperately wanted to talk to someone. Her stomach churning over the enormity of her actions, she poked out Renee's phone number.

"Married!" Renee squealed in Carly's ear. "That's— that's kind of sudden, isn't it?"

Carly had expected this reaction from her friend. Panic still fluttered in her stomach as she quickly capsulized the situation, ending with, "So it made sense."

"But—" Carly imagined Renee's eyebrows veeing with puzzlement. "What do you know about him?"

There were scads of details about Alex that she didn't know. "He's caviar and Dom Perignon."

"No kidding?"

Carly noted that her friend sounded impressed.

"So how does a girl who likes peanuts and hot dogs and fruit punch fit into that life?"

"That's the big question, isn't it?"

"Carly, this is—"

"Insane," Carly said, finishing for her.

She heard Renee draw a deep breath. "You must know more. He could be one of those weirdos who seems so nice and normal but—"

Carly answered lightly, honestly, "I doubt that."

"There should be more."

"There is," Carly said softly. "There's Billy."

Chapter Eight

During the next week, a routine snuck up on them. The sound of Billy's disgruntled wail announced with more accuracy than an alarm clock when it was time to wake up. Except for a casual passing remark, Carly and Alex went out of their way to avoid each other.

Carly spent her time getting settled in. She even visited some old friends in San Francisco. As they greeted news of her marriage with happiness, she let them believe what they wanted. The truth was, Alex was keeping his distance from her. Night after night, he came home after ten. She thought the less time they spent together, the better. What bothered her most, though, revolved around the time he wasn't spending with Billy.

Carly frowned down at her hands as she laced her sneakers. The diamond engagement ring nestled snugly against the wedding band like a symbol of unity. Alex was her husband now. Spouses should be able to talk honestly to each other.

She finished lacing her sneakers for her morning run. Rising from the bed, she resolved to speak with him— calmly, dispassionately. Forget the kiss. Forget the memory of the heat of his mouth. Forget everything except that Billy needed both of them.

Opening the door, she saw Alex standing in the nursery doorway. Like her, he was dressed in running shorts and a T-shirt. Soaked with perspiration, his clothing confirmed he'd finished his morning run. Briefly, discreetly, her eyes roamed over well-formed muscles in his arms, a flat midsection and long, well-toned thighs. Disturbingly, it occurred to her that she'd married a hunk. "Billy is with Dora. He's in his playpen downstairs," she announced as he looked her way.

Alex surveyed the nursery again. It was wiser than looking at her, at too much of a view of slender legs so early in the morning. "You redecorated."

Was he upset? "You said I could. Do you like it?"

Upon seeing it, Alex had thought that she generated change faster than anyone he knew. The nursery was bright and cheerful now. On a wall was a plaque of red and yellow and blue balloons. The wallpaper border contained a design of red and yellow stripes and a strip of dancing bears with balloons. A huge *ABC* hung above one dresser while on another was a lamp with two soft-looking teddy bears and a lamp shade in similar bright-colored stripes. From the comforter with the same brilliant colors to the curtains with a fabric alive with miniature balloons, the room vibrated with visual stimulation. "Does he?" Alex asked instead of answering her.

Carly thought that one response revealed a lot of the man she'd only glimpsed, who'd turned his world upside down for a child, who'd searched for a stuffed animal because it was his son's favorite, who'd married a woman he hardly knew to secure his job and a stable future for his child. "I think he does."

Alex eyed her yellow sneakers. "I didn't know you ran in the morning."

What they knew about each other would fill a thimble. "When my brother died, I stopped because I would have had to make arrangements for someone to watch Billy." She might seem scattered simply because she believed in spontaneity, because impulse ruled her, but she also needed routine and some guarantees in her life. "Alex, could we—"

"What?" he asked distractedly, glancing at his watch.

Carly knew the moment was wrong for a serious talk. "Nothing."

"Have a good day, then."

Carly sighed with his departure. Hardly scintillating or normal conversation for a husband and his wife. But what was normal about any of this?

At a quicker tempo than usual, she hit the running trail that wound its way through the woods. By the time she finished her run, she had only minutes to shower and change. As expected, Billy awoke from a nap with a demand for breakfast.

Wandering toward the kitchen with him, Carly heard voices and feminine laughter. She pushed at the swinging door and stepped into what she assumed was a coffee klatch between Dora and a petite and grandmotherly woman.

"I'm Adele Bridelman. Your neighbor. I live across the small pond." Smiling, the woman swiveled toward the kitchen's bay window and pointed to a Victorian house beyond the huge landscaped lawns.

Carly sat Billy in his high chair, then opened a jar of applesauce for him. With a look away from placing the contents in a bowl, she nearly drooled over the plate of luscious-looking homemade doughnuts the octogenarian had set on the table.

"She's my Tuesday buddy," Dora informed Carly. "We go to the racetrack."

Carly thought the sweet Adele and gruff Dora an unlikely pair, but then, wouldn't people view her and Alex as mismatched, too? "Who wins the most?" she asked while spooning the fruit into Billy's mouth.

"I do," they answered in unison, then laughed.

Loquacious, Adele dropped to a seat across from Carly and chatted on about her late husband who'd secured his money in oil. "When he got tired of business, he sold everything. Just like that," she added, snapping her fingers. "We traveled then until he died eight years ago. I was kind of lonely until Dora moved in here."

Dora paused in slicing herself an apple. "Others might say I was a bad influence."

"Phooey." Adele shook her head, then leaned conspiratorially close to Carly and whispered, "I always liked betting on the horses." A smile crinkled her face. "Did you know Dora was married to a jockey?"

"Only for a few months." The paring knife in her hand, Dora picked seeds from the apple. "I was too young to know better. All of eighteen. I wised up after that."

"You shouldn't be saying such things to her," Adele admonished. "Here she is with a little baby." She peered over the rim of the granny glasses perched on the bridge of her nose. "She should want to be married." Adele's eyes shifted to Billy. "And he is such a beautiful little boy."

"No." Carly laughed. "You have the wrong idea. We are married, but—" As Billy attempted to plunge his fingers into the mushy substance, she slid the bowl out of his reach, then clarified her relationship with Billy.

"His aunt," the woman said thoughtfully. Her dark eyes stayed on Billy. "He does look like his father. When I've sat outside, I would see Mr. Kane occasionally."

As Carly dabbed a damp washcloth at Billy's mouth, he grunted a protest and squirmed to avoid it. Five years Alex had been neighbors with Adele. Surely he must have made contact with this amiable woman at some time. "You really don't know Alex?"

With Carly's quizzical glance at Dora, she shrugged. "He's busy."

Humor slid into Adele's voice. "Even more now that he's a newlywed. I had hoped, though, that you were living together." The woman's eyes twinkled. "I was looking for hot gossip."

Carly laughed, deciding the stark white, sterile-looking kitchen had brightened considerably since Adele had walked in.

"Don't you have enough to keep you busy?" Dora asked the woman while pouring coffee for all of them.

Adele's smile waned. "Yes. The last time *he* called, he said that I'd better sell my property to him. And his voice kind of hung in the air like I should guess what he wasn't saying," Adele told them in a voice suddenly shaky with emotion.

Grabbing a doughnut, Carly took a quick bite. "He?" She zeroed in on the woman's pear-shaped face. "Who is he?" she asked while wiping a napkin across the powder sugar on the tips of her fingers.

"Vestor. That's all I know."

Alternately, the two older women explained that Adele owned several acres of valuable property on the ocean, and unlike other buyers, the man named Vestor wasn't taking no for an answer to his offer.

"What did you tell him the last time he called?" Carly asked, feeling a protective instinct emerge for a woman who was old enough to be her grandmother.

"I refused. Just as I did before." Nervously, Adele ran a smoothing hand over the napkin before her on the table. "But he's frightening me." She turned her eyes up at Dora. "He is, Dora."

"You said the property is valuable," Carly said.

"Oh, my, yes."

Carly hunched forward to untie Billy's bib. "And his offer was low, I bet."

"Indeed."

"Did he actually threaten you?"

Adele's forehead knitted. "I don't suppose I would say that, but he sounded quite menacing."

That wouldn't help with the police, Carly determined. "If he comes again, you call me." Carly caught Dora's raised eyebrow and chose to ignore it. She guessed Dora's thoughts. Alex wouldn't approve. He kept his life compartmentalized. He liked everything proper. Practical-minded, he would take the safe, cautious route and not get involved with some tough who used scare tactics. Differences. Sometimes they seemed almost insurmountable between them.

A smile returning to her face, Adele slipped a wrinkled hand over Carly's. "What a sweet thing to say."

Dora slanted a look at them. "You don't have to, Carly. I already promised Adele that I'll be there for her."

"Yes, she did." Adele nodded. "And I'm so grateful. I would hate to face him alone."

As Dora led Adele in contemplation of a good horse for the day's first race, Carly lifted Billy from his high chair. Whether Alex liked it or not, she knew if Adele had no one else, she would have kept that promise. She couldn't imagine turning her back on anyone.

While wandering outside days ago, to her delight, Carly had found a garden shed at the back of Alex's property. After Alex had left, she'd gotten a broom and bucket and cleaning solution from Dora and had spent the afternoon brushing away spiderwebs, sweeping out dust and scrubbing the walls and the floor.

For days, she'd been filled with the need to create, to feel wet clay beneath her fingers. She also needed to make a living. Despite the agreement with Alex, she didn't plan to live off of him.

Eager to get her equipment organized, she set Billy in his playpen outside the shed. Though the space was small and stuffy, she was grateful for a place to call her workshop. With Dora's help, she'd already moved a bench from the garage to use as a worktable. Its two drawers held her turning tools and calipers and shoe-mender's knife, and the drills and awl. She'd also found a metal utility cabinet with four shelves for greenware and bisqueware. While she needed more room for cones and the scales and glazing material, by late afternoon, she felt fatigued but pleased with what she'd accomplished.

Joining Billy, she viewed the flower garden, so much like the one she'd seen every summer while growing up. A chilling reprimand flashed back at her. She'd picked some of the flowers, certain a bouquet would please her aunt. Instead of pleasure, the woman had been furious when she'd seen them.

"Look at them but don't touch," her aunt had ordered.

At ten, Carly had nodded obediently. Never again had she looked at that garden with admiration.

Life wouldn't be like that for Billy. Children needed to explore, to play. She wanted the best of everything for him, but she wanted him to feel no restrictions when he wanted to laugh or run. Most of all, she wanted him to feel free to be himself, and to feel love.

Instead of eating dinner with Dora, Carly waited. Tonight was going to be different, she resolved. She was going to wait for Alex's return home. And they were going to talk.

By nine, her hunger long past, she slapped together a peanut butter and jelly sandwich.

At eleven, the glare of headlights from Alex's car shone against one of the living room windows. During the past hour, Carly had thumbed through a stack of magazines while dealing with an attack of annoyance. If late nights at the office remained a pattern for him, she wondered when Billy would see his father. It was *the* question on her mind when Alex opened the front door. Her feet planted, Carly stood in the living room's arched doorway. "Coffee's still hot," she insisted, to force him to join her.

Tired, Alex considered refusing. He'd deliberately stayed late at the office though nothing urgent had kept him there.

While Carly planned to have her say, she noted his hesitation and wondered if the moment might be more difficult than she'd expected. "I'll pour you a cup." With his reluctant nod of agreement, she let out a little breath of relief and hurried to the tray holding the carafe. "I wondered. Are you always going to be this late?"

Alex stopped at the foyer table and picked up the stack of mail. "Sometimes, I will be," he answered distractedly.

"But not always?"

"Not always." Because he'd promised her time, a promise he planned to keep, he'd thought avoiding cozy dinners made sense. The more he was around her, the more he would have to face the fact that he wanted her. So he relied on logic. For the agreement of a wife in name only to work, he needed to stay clear of her.

"That's good," Carly said, grabbing his attention again.

Alert to her verbal tiptoeing, Alex ended his perusal of the mail. Something else was happening. This whole scene revolved around more than her eagerness to perform some wifely act like pouring him coffee.

Carly nearly squirmed beneath the eyes narrowing as if they were trying to see what wasn't visible. "Because if you leave before dawn every day and come home with the vampires—"

"With the vampires?"

She heard amusement in his voice and waved a hand at him. "It's a figure of speech, Alex," she said with a trace of irritation. "Anyway, the important thing is that you haven't seen Billy all day." On a roll, she barely took a breath. "You need to be here for him."

Frowning now, Alex said, "What has you so riled up?"

"You." There was more truth in that than she wanted to face. "You have certain responsibilities."

Alex dropped the mail back onto the table.

"Billy needs more attention—from *you.*"

As if she'd punched him, his head snapped up. "He'll get plenty of that and more."

"More?" Carly heard the irritation accenting his voice. Anger had never been easy for her. Though she could be as stubborn as anyone, she usually shied away from confrontation. Too many harsh words, unforgivable words, slipped out when people were caught in the heat of anger. But she couldn't stop this time. "What does that mean?"

In his whole life, Alex had never backed down from a challenge, and she sure as hell was delivering one. "It means that it's taken me a lot of time to get where I am professionally." Despite his quiet tone, he drilled an intense stare at her.

"So you struggled?" she said.

"No, not struggle," he retorted, tugging at his tie. "I survived the odds to get here. To let up now would be foolish."

A need to understand skittered through her. "I don't know what you've gone through."

"It doesn't matter. What counts is that Billy will benefit from what I can give him."

If he'd explained, she would have been more under-standing. Instead, her frustration intensified. "Billy needs love more than money." Who knew that better than her? "If you don't give him that, then you're giv-ing him nothing."

"Wait a minute."

Carly stood firm. "No, you wait. I'm not done." How could such an intelligent man be so dense? she wondered, meeting his stare squarely. "All I know is, either be a father full-time or let me take him. He doesn't need someone who only *might* be here for him," she told him. "A child needs his father, needs to know he can depend on him."

Alex sucked in a breath as her words hit home—hard.

Furious, Carly opened her mouth to speak, but nothing came out. He looked as if she'd punched him and knocked the wind from him. "Alex—"

"I'm going outside." He couldn't say more. She'd revived an onslaught of memories. The moment he stepped through the French doors, he drew in a deep breath. He needed the cool, fresh air of evening. He needed to remember who he was as an old wound fes-tered as if it were inflicted on him yesterday instead of decades ago.

Stunned, Carly stared after him. Anguish. She'd seen it in his eyes. What had she said to cause it? Indecisive, she stood in the middle of the living room. Should she leave him alone? How could she? He was hurting. She didn't know why, but she needed to.

Quietly, she followed to stop feet from him. "I know you've worked hard," she said softly because she was at a loss. As his shoulders heaved with what seemed a weary sigh, Carly tried again. "I know being a father is new to you."

It scared the hell out of Alex. Women took to mothering naturally, but for a man, a manual of instructions should come with the job.

"But you're the one he'll look to." She wanted to say more, to make him listen.

"For what?"

His question shocked her. Every time he held Billy, she'd seen how capable he was of loving. "For all the things fathers and sons do," she said, though she thought that was obvious. "Play ball. Whatever... Think back. What did you do with your father?"

Foolishly, Alex had thought the past was behind him. Except for Dora, no one knew, no one would guess that it controlled every fiber of his being. "I never knew him."

As if cold water had been tossed at her, Carly mentally faltered. "Never?"

Alex shook his head. "Not really. He left when I was two or three. I don't know."

Instinctively, because reaching out to others was as natural to her as breathing, she stepped closer and slid her hand over his. "And your mother?"

He stared with distant eyes as if he were somewhere else. "My mother. She was there, sort of," he said on a mirthless laugh. "She didn't cope well with problems." Alex cursed himself. He couldn't veil the bitterness. It filled him, and even as he resisted, it poured out of him now. "After I was born, she went back to finding solace in alcohol, and he left her. That's all," he murmured, amazed he'd told her that much.

"Don't do that," Carly appealed.

"You want it all?" Anger darkened his eyes. "Okay. Their marriage was shaky to begin with, and neither of them wanted to stick it out. I didn't matter. My father abandoned us, and before my fifth birthday, I knew I couldn't count on her, either, for anything. She proved me right. She took off before I turned twelve."

Carly's heart twisted for the hurt he'd endured. "What happened then?" she asked softly, linking her fingers with his.

Her touch nearly undid him. He'd always been alone. He'd thought he hadn't cared, hadn't wanted anyone else. He still wasn't sure he did.

"What happened then?" she repeated.

"What you would expect." More memories snuck in on him, some bad, few good. "Foster care. I took off when I was fifteen." Alex raised his eyes to her. Even beneath the moonlight, he could see a flicker of uneasiness stirring a frown line between her eyebrows.

Not wanting to let him pull away now, Carly tightened her grip on his hand. "And did what?"

He'd skirted the law. "I drifted," Alex answered because that was enough. "I don't know why I went back to the old neighborhood, but I did. A neighbor petitioned the court to take me in. It was Dora."

How lucky he'd been to find her was Carly's only thought. "A special lady."

"Yeah," he practically whispered.

The slender thread of trust between them lengthened enough for Carly to ask, "So when you got all this, you hired her?"

Alex forced a smile. What she'd said was so far from the truth. "She's not an employee, Carly. She's family. She's all I've ever had."

He had more now, but it would take time for him to accept that, Carly realized.

"She refused to come with me if I hired someone to keep house when she could do it," he explained. "I figured I owed her. I was an angry kid, but—" he offered a strained grin "—smart. I knew hard work was my ticket away from all that." For a long moment, Alex stared at her. What he saw nearly undermined him. He'd expected inquisitiveness, or worse, sympathy. Instead, he saw understanding. It was the one thing he hadn't expected.

It didn't take much for Carly to envision how hard he'd struggled to have so much. "You've come far." She sensed now he'd never gotten past the feeling that if he eased up on his work, everything he had might slip away. With the moonlight slanting across his face, she saw a darkness in his eyes that carried so much sadness she ached. "How much did you have to sacrifice?"

Everything, Alex mused. No, nothing. He'd never had anything except his work. Resentment and hurt had made him battle to succeed. He'd done it all on his own, had never counted on anyone else. "Whatever I gave up was worth it."

Carly wondered if that was true. "This time it won't be." She knew how capable he was of tenderness, how giving he could be if he let himself be. "This time you'll get more than you'll give up. Reach out for Billy," she urged. "He's there for you, Alex. If there's anything in this world you can count on, it's that he'll love you if you let him."

His head raised slowly. In his eyes, she saw confusion. Carly released a soft sigh. He was dealing with too much hurt for her to prod him anymore. As his hand slipped from hers and he turned away, she was at a loss for how to reach him. Unless he opened his heart to his son, they would both lose.

Alex ran a hand over his face. Tired, he wondered why she, of all the people he'd ever met, had drawn all that from him. No longer teased by her fragrance, he sensed she'd left.

He moved his shoulders to ease the tension there. All his life, he'd pulled back from people. It had been safer to depend on only himself, to expect nothing from anyone else. He'd relied on his work to fill his world. She was asking him to rethink his whole way of life. She was forcing him to question everything he'd been so certain about—until now.

He couldn't argue against what made so much sense. He'd stayed away because of her, but Billy was the one being hurt by his actions. And there was the reminder that had nearly rocked him. It seemed he was more his parents' son than he realized. Avoiding anything that might be difficult had always been their way. And it hadn't mattered who was hurt as long as they weren't.

Foolishly, he'd thought himself better than them. It was an awareness of his own accountability that had sent him in search of his son. But had he screwed up after that? Like everything in his life, hadn't he accepted fatherhood as another achievement, and nothing more? But it should be more, a damn lot more.

Who knew that better than him? As a child, he'd endured emptiness and loneliness; if what she was saying proved true, his son would endure the same. He couldn't let that happen.

Alex swore softly. If he wasn't like his parents, it was time to prove it; it was time to bury old ghosts.

A stirring inside him to see his son made him stroll back to the house. "I'll do better," he murmured, though no one heard him but himself.

Carly thought avoiding Alex might be best. But ever since waking, she'd wondered if anything she'd said to him had penetrated. She knew she needed to see him, and at least arrange a truce, if that was necessary.

A peace offering in her hand, she opened the door to leave her bedroom. Her heart thudding with both surprise and apprehension, Carly moved the hand with her peace offering behind her back.

He stood before her, dressed except for his suit jacket, his hand behind him.

Expecting some measure of anger from him, she dramatically squared her shoulders. Apologies were never easy, but he deserved one. She'd forced moments on him that she was sure he'd have preferred to avoid. "About last night, I shouldn't have—"

"Yes, you should have," Alex cut in. Amazingly, he felt more at peace. He would always wonder if it might have come sooner if someone before this had forced him to talk about the past. No one had until her. For that and for the wake-up call about his son, he owed her a lot. "I'm sorry. You were right."

"I was?"

Her astonished look made him smile. "You were."

"You're not angry?"

He'd been damn angry. She'd been intrusive and painfully honest. "I was, but thank you. And these aren't much, but they're for you."

Dumbfounded, Carly stared at a bouquet of daisies and peonies and mums. Her heart hammered. Never would she have expected him to pick flowers for a woman. "You picked them?"

Alex thought her question strange. He owed her much more. "Shouldn't I have?"

He had no idea how much the sight of those flowers weakened her. "They're so pretty," she said softly, remembering how she'd stood before the garden and admired the abundance of flowers.

Carly gave herself another moment of enjoyment, then brought her hand around from her back and presented him with her offering of peace. "And this is for you."

Alex stared down at what he thought at first was a shallow porcelain dish. But after a moment, he could see that her hands and mind had been more inspired. The simple lines of the pottery disguised the intricacy of achievement involved in shaping it like a seashell.

"It's for your office. If you want to take it there." Nerves stirred within her at his quietness. "I hope you like it."

"Like it?" Alex traded her the flowers for the pottery. It was beautiful, fragile and delicate-looking with its crisp irregular edge. "Thank you. But why?"

She knew now he hadn't received much in life. "Because you gave me this ring and I didn't have anything for you. And it was a peace offering," she admitted.

"It's beautiful." His fingers brushed her cheek with a touch that was so gentle, she nearly swayed into it. "Thank you."

Carly had wanted to impress. What she hadn't expected was such a swift surge of pleasure at pleasing him. "And I thought you would want this." She set a small gold-framed photograph in his hand and stepped into the hallway with him. "We hope you like it."

Alex smiled instinctively. In the photograph, his son grinned back at him in a manner Alex remembered at their first meeting. Wasn't it then the ties had been formed? Wasn't it then one little boy had inched into his heart? At that moment, Alex had known he wasn't leaving without him. "Carly—" Looking up, he saw that he was talking to himself. He needed to say more, but she was halfway down the stairs.

Again, he stared down at her gifts, one made with care and the other meant to remind him to do just that with his son.

Chapter Nine

At the bottom of the stairs, Alex heard the phone ring and detoured around the front door. He hit the swinging door of the kitchen in time to see Dora cradling the receiver between her jaw and shoulder.

"Try and stop me," she was announcing to the caller. Spotting Alex standing in the doorway, she held up a finger in a gesture requesting him to wait. "I'll be there by the weekend."

As she set the receiver back in its cradle, Alex ended his distracted viewing of Carly strolling in the garden. "Is something wrong?"

"I need to leave for a while. My sister—"

"Which one?"

"The one who lives in Maine. The klutzy one. Gertrude. Even as a girl, she was always knocking things over. She broke her hip. Stepped off a curb and fell. So she needs someone to stay with her.''

"Then go." Despite Dora's disgusted tone about her sister's clumsiness, Alex had learned long ago that her sisters meant the world to her.

"Will you be all right here without me?"

"Probably not," he said, because he knew she would want to hear that. "But we'll manage until you get back." He swept a look around the kitchen.

Flowerpots filled with greenery hung from the ceiling over the bay window seat. He noticed the plain gray-and-white fabric that had formerly covered it had been replaced with one that had a bright yellow-and-gray design. Short matching curtains, which were pulled back to let in the full morning sunlight, adorned the window, and on an adjacent wall was a reproduction of Van Gogh's *Sunflowers*.

"Your kitchen has been invaded, I see," Alex said lightly, liking the room's new sunny appearance.

"She has a green thumb."

"How did this happen in such short time?"

"She's a bundle of energy. I'll give her that." Dora poured him a cup of coffee and cracked a grin at him. "Nice improvement, isn't it?"

"Different."

Dora smirked as she set the cup on the table.

Alex prepared himself for her opinion. Instead, she whipped away and flung open the refrigerator door. He eyed the white take-out cartons that were synonymous with Chinese food. "I thought you hated Chinese food."

"It's for her breakfast."

"Breakfast?" Alex shook his head, then walked away, laughing.

Every time he looked up from his desk that day, his eyes strayed either to his son's photograph or to the seashell pottery. He hadn't considered what he would begin to feel with Carly near all the time.

At first, he'd intended nothing more than a business arrangement. He'd analyzed the situation briefly and had come to the conclusion that she wasn't his type. He liked predictable. He always wanted to know what to expect. Always.

Back then, she'd wanted to stay with Billy, and he'd wanted to take his son home.

Simple objectives.

They'd married under similar terms.

Not the smartest thinking, though, for an executive used to establishing practical long-term goals.

He'd completely ignored the possibility that he might begin to care about her, that he might want more than a marriage in name only or that he would be obsessed with thoughts of making love with her.

Her spirits higher than usual, Carly drove to the city to find another potter who would agree to let her use his kiln. She supposed it was the soaring optimism generated by Alex's attitude that morning that made her drive by her aunt's home. After everything he'd told her about his childhood, she found herself wondering about the only family she'd ever had. Briefly she'd envisioned a family reunion complete with apologies and a dinner invitation from her aunt. It was a silly daydream. She knew it would never happen.

Refusing to allow her mood to droop, she indulged in a lunch of what Alex would consider junk food. She finished off a fast-food hamburger and fries and a gooey fudge brownie, then spent several hours at the studio of a fellow potter. Though thrilled at his agreeing to let her use his kiln, she knew she would have to invest in one herself soon.

For someone who'd never worried about money while growing up, she found it required a lot of her attention now. Any money she'd previously saved, she'd used to care for Billy, and until she began selling her pottery again, she would be cash short. As much as she wanted a kiln, she would never ask Alex for it.

By the time she returned home, the sun was nearing the horizon. Cradling Billy in her arm, she opened the kitchen door to the sound of chimes from the grandfather clock. It signaled six o'clock. Carly assumed she would have another evening alone after feeding Billy. One step in, and she learned she was wrong.

Standing at the refrigerator with a bottle of wine in his hand, Alex swung a look back at her. "Hi."

An idiotic grin curved her lips. He'd come home early. He really had listened to her. "Hi, yourself. Have you been home long?"

"An hour." He discovered he liked the idea of being alone with her and his son in the kitchen. During his youth, he'd seen a Norman Rockwell painting of a family of three, sitting in a kitchen together. The painting had delivered a simple message of warmth and coziness. Alex had thought it illustrated the way a family should be. Closing the refrigerator door, he stirred from his thoughts to see Carly setting Billy's carrier seat on the floor. "Where's Dora?"

"At the dentist's." She handed Billy a set of plastic keys. With a look up, she saw Alex scowling at the refrigerator as if it were evil personified. "Is there a problem?"

He sort of winced. "Friends are coming for dinner. Dora always makes too much or I wouldn't have invited them without calling her first."

"So I'll cook."

He gave her a half-amused look. "Carly, I don't expect you to cook for them." How could he? Though married, the usual rules didn't apply between them. What's more, he had doubts about her culinary expertise.

"Billy's too tired to take out to dinner." Her back to him, Carly opened the freezer door and eyed the giant-size beef roast, the roasting chicken, the leg of lamb, some ground beef. She had no idea what to cook. What could she thaw quickly in the microwave? "There's no one to watch him. And what restaurant that your friends would like would welcome a baby?"

Still, Alex was hesitant. "What would you make?"

Carly closed her fingers over the hamburger. "A surprise." She swung around to see Alex frowning. She supposed his friends were used to haute cuisine.

"A surprise?"

Ignoring the doubt in his voice, Carly shoved the hamburger in the microwave, then set a pan of water for noodles on a burner. "I'll make Veronica's stroganoff."

"Veronica?"

"She lived on the third floor in my apartment building." Carly bent forward and rummaged in the vegetable crisper of the refrigerator. "She read tarot cards."

"Look, Carly, they're used to—"

She gave a little sigh. She shouldn't have expected him to change overnight, but it would have pleased her if he wasn't revealing so much concern about what others might think.

As she turned a frown back at him, Alex curbed what he'd planned to say. At the moment, he only cared about seeing her smile again. Whatever she made would be fine, he decided. "I like surprises."

There was hope for him, she mused. A carton of sour cream in her hands, she matched his smile. "What time are they coming?"

"Seven-thirty." Alex skirted the table to move closer. "We're going to have to play husband and wife one night next week." His fingers trailed over her hand that was holding the carton. "Some business associates expect to be invited over to celebrate our marriage."

Tingling from his caress, Carly fought to register what he'd said. This time, she was the one unnerved about what impression she would make. "Here?"

He brushed aside her question as he realized he only had to ease forward to sample her lips. "Don't worry."

But Carly was worried. Worried about the way he was studying her and the way his look was warming her blood. Worried that love might sneak in. The last time she'd believed in love, it had been with a man like Alex, and she'd been struck down. Worried, too, because it would be so easy to lean closer, to raise her mouth to his. So easy.

She didn't have to do anything. His mouth was suddenly on hers. Unhurried, his lips coaxed and persuaded for only a second, but it was long enough for her to feel needs rising, to send tingling sparks shooting through her. Still breathless, she swayed back against the kitchen counter. Only then did she hear the doorbell. "Alex—"

His mouth hovered near once more. "I heard it," he murmured, but he could barely think about anything but the taste of her. For a few seconds, all reason had fled. Skimming her arm, he stopped at her wrist. Beneath his fingers, he felt her pulse hammering.

As the doorbell chimed again, Carly placed a hand to his chest. To stop him or herself? She wasn't sure. "What do we do tonight?" she managed to ask softly.

He met eyes that were darker, more intense with emotion. Not quite steady himself, Alex took a second before answering, "Pretend."

Everything seemed a touch out of kilter to Carly. "You don't mean that."

"Yes, I do." Alex could imagine the shock his friends would register if he announced the marriage had nothing to do with love. He stepped away while he still could, but paused in the doorway and braced a hand against the doorjamb to look back at her. She looked baffled. By his kiss or his words? he wondered. "They would be upset to learn this was anything but the real thing."

Carly couldn't veil her incredulity. "Do you really expect them to believe this? We met only a short time ago."

"They'll believe love at first sight," Alex assured her. At least Julia with her romantic nature would. Doug would nail him with questions later.

Alone, Carly slouched against the counter. Because she still felt shaky, for good measure, she reminded herself they didn't exactly have a love match. It would be stupid to get carried away by romantic notions. It really would be.

Though meeting new people rarely bothered her, while she finished up in the kitchen, she fretted about the evening ahead. What if his friends were like her cousin Christian's? They would hardly be impressed with a dinner meant for a pinching-pennies budget. Despite her confidence around Alex, she crossed her fingers about dinner.

And she worried about that party next week. She remembered the brunette who'd visited him, the perfect type for a rising young executive's wife. She couldn't banish old ghosts, ones that tauntingly haunted her with insecurities.

Minutes later, she had water boiling and was stirring sour cream into the cooked ground beef and cream of mushroom soup mixture. Satisfied with her progress, she quickly slipped upstairs to change. After giving Billy a bottle, she tucked him in bed. Half-a-dozen deep breaths later, she descended the staircase.

"I should punch you," she heard a man say good-naturedly from the living room. "I can't believe you got married."

Carly felt smug. She'd told Alex they would never believe his love-at-first-sight act, hadn't she?

"We're thrilled," a woman said. "I just knew when you met the right woman that you would make a snap decision."

Carly mentally groaned.

The woman's voice softened. "And you found your son, too? That's so wonderful, Alex."

Butterflies taking flight in her stomach, Carly slowly crossed the foyer.

An attractive blond couple sat with Alex on the sofas near the fireplace.

"We were dying to come," the woman said. "I wanted to meet her, and to see the baby."

"She couldn't wait," the man teased, gesturing with his thumb in his wife's direction.

"No, I couldn't," she said cheerfully and unabashedly.

Carly waited at the perimeter. What did Alex's friends really think of her sudden appearance in his life? Suddenly, she felt very alone, standing in his house, a stranger to his friends.

The woman's eyes strayed and met Carly's. "Hi, I'm Julia."

Carly nudged herself to step closer and accept the woman's hand.

Tall, thin and intelligent-looking, she exuded finishing-school charm. Wearing a designer silk outfit, she was definitely not the type to appreciate hamburger for dinner.

Playing the smitten husband to the hilt, Alex curled his fingers around Carly's waist and tugged her close. "Sweetheart, this is Doug and Julia Dalton. Old friends." He inclined his head so his breath heated her cheek. The casual act cost him dearly. With her pressed so close, he felt the softness of her breast rub against him with each breath she drew.

"Ooh, I hate that word—*old*." Julia feigned a shudder. "We went to college with Alex. And he—" She paused, her eyes narrowing at Carly. "You know, you look familiar. Have we met?"

Still glued to Alex's side, Carly plastered a smile on her face while she tried not to think how amazingly strong he felt. He runs and works out, she reminded herself. Annoyance skittered through her as a betraying thought made her wonder if his muscles would ripple beneath her hands. "I don't think so." The moment felt too real. Like a besotted bridegroom, he kept his possessive iron grip on her and kissed her cheek. To anyone watching, they looked in love.

"It's so great meeting you," Julia murmured. "I can stop worrying about him now." She gestured at Alex, then hooked her arm in Carly's. "Can we see the baby?" she pleaded.

Carly nodded. Still heady, she didn't trust herself to say too much.

Fortunately, Julia took control of the conversation as the four of them climbed the stairs. "Doug and I met Alex in college. He was so brooding and solemn-faced, so serious that we felt sorry for him," Julia teased. "So we sat down and talked to him."

Beside Doug, Alex followed them up the stairs. "And I haven't been able to get rid of them since," he said affectionately.

"Tough," Doug mumbled.

With a glance back at them, Julia laughed then spoke conspiratorially to Carly, "They really do like each other."

Carly hadn't needed her assurance. Their camaraderie bespoke a naturalness that came only from years of friendship.

"Oh," Julia gushed the moment she reached the crib. "He's beautiful. Oh, Alex." She spun a look on him. "You must be proud."

Alex discovered that he was—of Billy and of the woman he called his wife.

Throughout the meal, his gaze fastened on Carly. She brightened the room with her light spirit, sharing humorous stories about Billy and intelligently discussing impressionist artists with Doug. Alex thought again about the schooling she'd had. Who was she, really? he wondered not for the first time since Bennett Doleman had dropped his bombshell about her family.

The questions Carly had anticipated Alex's friends would ask never came. Instead, Julia had rambled on about her and Doug's law firm, about her hope that soon they would have their own child. Even more impressive, they ate more than one helping of her meal.

"Dinner was wonderful," Julia assured her, then laughed. "Carly, I know we've met—" Julia stopped midsentence, looking startled. "Oh, dear."

Both men raised their heads.

"What's up?" Doug asked.

"Nothing." Julia pretended interest in smoothing the napkin on her lap.

Alex chuckled. "Out with it."

"Forget it," Julia returned through barely moving lips.

"How can we?" her husband answered. "You've aroused our curiosity."

Carly had to admit her curiosity was piqued, too.

Julia sent her a quick apologetic look. "I hate doing this to newlyweds."

Carly didn't have the vaguest idea what she was talking about.

"Carly, we met at the country club about ten years ago." At Carly's frown, she went on, "You were celebrating your engagement to Austin Westerly."

The third, Alex mused.

Carly twisted the napkin in her lap. She'd worked so hard to forget that time in her life.

Julia made a face. "I'm sorry for bringing that up, Alex."

"The past isn't important," he said, but it suddenly was to him. He was married to the woman across the table from him, and he knew nothing about her.

"So you'll come for dinner one night next week," Julia insisted later when they stood at the door.

"I would love to," Carly answered and meant it.

"And you can give me that recipe." Julia's eyes gleamed with an impish sparkle. "I can hardly wait to serve it to my in-laws," she said in another conspiratorial whisper. "They are so...so dignified. You know what I mean."

Only too well. Carly had been raised by the same pretentious type of people.

"I'll call you," Doug said before they departed.

As Alex closed the door, possessively he skimmed Carly's neck with a fingertip.

"They were nice," Carly said honestly and hurried from his touch to the table to clear away the dishes.

Alex followed. It was reasonable that he would want her so much. With a look or touch, desire repeatedly crackled between them. So why did a woman who possessed so much warmth and revealed such depth of caring for others keep herself at a distance from him? It was time for him to learn more about a past that included some guy with the blueblood name of Austin Westerly III. "You're a natural hostess." Across the table from her, he stacked plates. "But then, none of that is new to you, is it? The Criswells were known for their gala parties."

The silverware Carly had gathered nearly slipped from her fingers. "How did you know?" She met his stare. "Did you check me out?"

"For what it's worth, I never checked on your background, Carly. Others with an interest in my success told me that you're Arden Criswell's daughter and the granddaughter of Lionel Criswell."

"And so forth, and so forth." Carly clutched the silverware and scooted into the kitchen.

Alex had no intention of backing off.

At the click of his heels across the kitchen floor, Carly tensed. "Are you trying to understand how I could come from such a well-mannered background?"

"Stop right now," Alex retorted. "I'm not judging anything. I'm the last person who would. Where you came from doesn't mean anything to me, and for good reason. I dragged myself up. You know that. I've worked a damn long time to make sure no one remembers my background."

Eyes dark and shadowed met his. "So have I," she admitted softly.

Again, she stood with her back ramrod straight. Alex stepped forward and slipped the dish towel from her hand. "Come on," he urged and led her into the living room.

Carly felt like running. It stunned her that the mere mention of all that she'd left behind could still open her raw. She'd fought hard to stand alone, to move away from her aunt and uncle, to reject an inbred yearning for their approval. And she hadn't wanted to be reminded of what she'd excised from her life years ago. "So what are you thinking?"

Alex considered how many layers of her existed. He'd seen strength, determination, humor and now vulnerability. "I'm wondering why you didn't ask your family for help when you needed it," he said, drawing her down with him to the sofa.

Uneasy, she breathed deeply. "I never would."

"What about your brother? Why didn't he leave you anything to make life easier?" As she sighed, Alex sensed she wanted him to back off. He couldn't, not yet.

"What Randy left is Billy's, not mine." The last thing she wanted was to dwell on the past, but she forced herself to offer an explanation, certain it was the only way to cease his questions. "When I was eight, my parents died. My brother was eleven. That's when we went to live with my aunt and uncle. Stiff, inflexible, disapproving people. They didn't understand children, didn't want to, but felt they had a responsibility."

Her description sounded so much like him that if Alex had heard it weeks ago, he would have squirmed.

"They gave my brother and me everything—almost." She'd learned about obedience and demands for her perfection. She'd learned that her own opinions and wishes hadn't mattered. She'd trained herself to follow rules. Mostly, she'd known about never fitting in. "You see, they had certain expectations that my brother and I didn't quite meet. I was too wild, too impulsive, too much of a tomboy."

Carly sighed with the memory of her last night in her aunt's house. Years of anger had exploded from her when her aunt had refused to discuss Carly's father. Before Carly had left the house, her aunt's voice had filled with quiet disdain. He was unproductive, a dreamer who only thought about pleasure. He was too improper for a Criswell. What her aunt hadn't said had come through clearly. *You're just like him.*

A building pressure in her chest reminded her of emotions and memories she'd left behind willingly. "I was too strong-willed, not ladylike enough. In their eyes, I never succeeded in being perfect enough, no matter how hard I tried." Raising her gaze to him, Carly attempted a smile. "As you can imagine, I never fit the mold of what they expected of me."

Alex skimmed his thumb over her knuckles. "Were they unkind?"

"No," she said quickly because it was the truth. "I'm grateful to them for what they gave us. They provided all of the creature comforts to my brother and me— more than that." A small frown carved a line between her eyebrows. "But everything had conditions." Unconsciously, Carly tilted her head back in a prideful move. "By the time I was eighteen, I wanted so badly to please them that I was willing to do anything." Despite the warmth in the house, she hugged herself as a chill swept over her. "So much so that I nearly invited disaster into my life. Austin was handpicked for me. He was perfect, according to my aunt. He would settle me down."

Alex frowned. *And take the spirit out of her.*

"I didn't know then that he was everything I didn't want in my life. All that mattered, I thought, was that everyone was pleased." Carly shifted and tucked her legs beneath her. "We'd been engaged two weeks, when I did the unthinkable. On the night of our official engagement party, it was raining and stormy. I don't know why I stepped outside, but I did. There was a stray cat, drenched and shivering. I went into the rain, cuddled the cat and brought it into the kitchen."

Alex's frown deepened as he tried to comprehend what she'd done so far that was so bad.

"I was soaked. Dressed to the nines for the party. Guests had already begun arriving. Austin came looking for me because the proper thing to do was to greet them. He was furious. I couldn't blame him—the hem of my dress was dirty, my hair was plastered to my head and a hundred people were waiting for us to appear at the party." Carly raised her head, expecting to see Alex's frown of disapproval.

He gave her a crooked grin. "You would have made a great entrance."

She laughed, and that surprised her. She'd never laughed when she'd thought about those days. "I didn't. I apologized to Austin. It wasn't enough. He and my aunt declared that I'd done the unforgivable."

"Couldn't you change clothes?"

"I did. But the guests had already seen me." She shrugged. "He wouldn't forgive me."

Narrow-minded bastard was Alex's first thought.

"I'd embarrassed him in front of his friends and relatives. My aunt felt the same."

"Carly, they overreacted. You hardly committed the crime of the century."

She hugged herself. "To their way of thinking, I had. Everything always had to be perfect. I wasn't. So Austin broke off the engagement." She offered another slim smile. "If he hadn't, I would have."

Alex studied her eyes for regret and was glad not to see any. Nothing lasts forever. He'd learned that lesson years ago. Obviously, so had she.

"Everything became clear that night. I didn't belong there. Didn't want to belong. So I left."

Alex doubted it was that simple.

"I didn't feel anything they offered was worth what they wanted me to give up. Who I was."

"What about your brother?"

"Randy had done better than me. He'd handled the restrictions. And at that time, he was away at college."

Alex slid his fingers over her hand. She looked sad, vulnerable. Wanting to reassure her, he almost drew her close. But he doubted she would want the sympathy. He understood her better now and why they'd been at odds. She thought he was like her family and the jerk she'd been engaged to. That's why she'd adamantly refused to let him have Billy. Perhaps it was also why he felt such wariness in her when he got too close. "Have you seen them since?" he asked softly.

"When my brother died, they came to the funeral. We exchanged a few words, but we're strangers.... They thought they'd given me everything. What they didn't understand is that they never gave what was most important. They never gave love."

Alex didn't regret asking, but he wished he hadn't whipped up a turmoil inside her.

"Everyone's got their hot button." Carly turned an apologetic smile up at him. "You found mine."

Alex shrugged. "I didn't mean to push it."

Her smile lingered. "It's funny how a word or two can stir reaction, isn't it?"

Tentatively, Alex toyed with her hair. As if binding them, one blond curl coiled around his finger. "Only if you let that happen."

How much she'd needed that reminder, she realized.

Unable to ignore her shuddery breath, he touched her shoulders. Someone with such a gentle soul hadn't deserved so much hurt. The need to comfort her overwhelmed him. He drew her into his arms, he stroked her hair, and with every breath he drew, her scent filled him with a memory of her sweetness.

It was the change in the way he was holding her that made Carly look up.

As if testing, he lightly brushed his lips across hers. Gentle. Tender. Only he had ever kissed her in such a way. Swaying closer, she placed a hand against his shoulder as the kiss deepened. Pleasure skittered through her. It took only a moment for everything else to be forgotten. Her mind emptied. Sensations rippling through her, she absorbed the taste and feel of him, welcomed the sweet, savoring play of his mouth. Within seconds, he spun her with a need for which she hadn't braced herself.

Beneath his mouth, her lips were warm and willing. Against him, her body was soft and pliant. Sheer pleasure whipped an urgency through her. Passion teased her.

She clung, responding, running her hand over the strong planes of his face. She struggled now not to moan and heard her own sigh. Ever since he'd kissed her the first time, a part of her had yearned to let herself be swept away with him.

But did they dare step over the ledge toward intimacy? What if at some moment love confused everything? If she loved him, she would be ripped apart when he turned from her. As he surely would. For at some unexpected moment, she would disappoint him and then lose him.

Battling herself more than him, she wedged a hand between them to end the kiss. "I'm not ready for this," she murmured breathlessly but couldn't move away.

For a long second, a quiet challenge stretched between them. Then, feather-light, he traced the outline of her lips. "You're ready," he said softly, huskily.

He was right. But she was afraid to believe in them, afraid of being hurt. Scrambling to a stand, she saw a flicker of impatience cross his face.

The staircase suddenly seemed miles away. Carly hurried to it even as she wanted to turn around and fling herself back in his arms, even as she yearned for what she'd just denied. Desire she could deal with, but what did she do about what he made her feel, made her long for again?

Chapter Ten

Alex awoke in a foul mood. Snatching up his brief-case, he wandered down the stairs. The phone had rung five times, once while he was showering, then while he was shaving, again when he was tying his tie and two more times since he'd left the bedroom. Not once had Dora yelled that he had a phone call. Entering the kitchen, he scanned the counter for phone messages. "I know I heard the phone."

Her eyes riveted on the odds for the afternoon's horse race, Dora held out a coffee cup to him. "Not for you."

Instead of taking the cup in passing, Alex paused before her. "None of them?"

"Nope."

"Were they for you?"

Shaking her head, Dora returned to the dishes she'd been washing. "Not me. Carly."

"I'm sorry," Carly said behind him. "Did the phone calls bother you?"

The only thing bothering him was her. As she stepped into the kitchen, rays of sunlight spiked through the curtain to highlight paler strands in her blond hair. Her skin glowed with rosiness, but she wore no makeup. Last night, he'd touched skin that had felt like velvet. He hadn't imagined her straining against him during the kiss, nor had he conjured up the aching need in her arms around his neck. Yet here they were back to square one.

"You need this," Dora insisted, forcing Carly around to accept a glass of orange juice. "Drink first."

Clutching Billy, Carly skirted past Alex. She'd slept miserably, waking often with thoughts of Alex. If only he didn't make her want to believe in something she'd nearly given up believing in years ago? Downing the glass of juice, she thought it best if she acted casual. It was the only way to get through this moment. "I have to run." Whether it was head-in-the-sand silliness or not, she thought if she dodged him now, she could pretend last night hadn't happened. "Thank you, Dora. Bye, Alex," she called out with a backhanded wave at him before dashing out the door.

Alex didn't buy her act. No way could she be unaffected, if the kiss had left him grabbing for breath. "Where is she going?"

Dora cackled lightly.

In no mood for her smug comments, Alex glowered at her. "Have you got a problem?"

"Not me," she sang out.

"So where is she going?"

"If today is Friday, she's off to collect books."

Alex planted his backside onto the edge of the table. Whether he would be late or not, he was determined to find out what was going on before he left. "Where is she collecting books?"

"She got the addresses over the phone."

"Dora," he said with exasperation, feeling as if the females in the house had formed a silent conspiracy, "why is she collecting books?"

Dora gave him a grin. "This being Friday—"

"We already established that."

"Then she's picking up the donations for the animal shelter fund-raiser. Now, if it were Monday, she would be on the street corner handing out pamphlets."

"What!" He bolted to a stand.

"When did you get so hard of hearing?"

"Don't be cute. Why is she handing out pamphlets?"

"Save the whales, dolphins, seals. I don't know."

"But it's one of them?"

Dora's eyes sparkled as they peered at him over the rim of her coffee cup. "Probably all of them. On Tuesdays though—" She paused, giving Alex time to drop back to the table edge.

"Tuesdays what?" he asked skeptically.

"She volunteers at the hospital day-care, and on Thursdays, she and Billy go to a fitness class for mothers and babies. Wednesday is when she usually spends time around here. She's organizing some kind of Block Watch."

Alex shook his head in amazement.

Dora set down her cup. "Interesting woman, isn't she?"

Fascinating suited her better. She loved his child as if he were her own. She brightened a room when she walked into it. She made passion boil within him.

Stepping outside, Alex groaned at the sight of a very seductive backside aimed at him while Carly secured Billy in his car seat.

"Going bye-bye," Carly sang to Billy. She shut the back door and tugged down her short skirt, then pivoted to slip behind the steering wheel. With one leg halfway in, she noticed Alex. Her plan to escape shriveled with his smile. "Did you want to talk to me?" The words sounded ridiculous even to her own ears.

Alex heard nerves in her voice and took the first step to close the distance between them. "I thought, if you're not busy, we could take Billy and spend time in the city. But you're busy."

Carly nodded dumbly. *We.* She eased her other leg out of the car and gripped the top edge of the car door to keep her legs steady. "Why?"

"We could consider it a thank-you for keeping me from making a mistake with my son. How about tomorrow?" As a warm breeze whirled around them, with a fingertip, he lifted away wisps of hair that were brushing her forehead. "What do you say?"

She would say she was in trouble. "Tomorrow's fine," she answered, nodding agreeably.

By the time she pulled back into the driveway, a sense of satisfaction filled Carly. Though she'd spent hours carting boxes filled with dusty books, she'd accomplished too much to mind the hard work or the dirtiness of the job.

She unloaded Billy's stroller from the trunk, then unsnapped him from his car seat. In her arms, he pumped his legs and hummed. "You have a new sound," she said, laughing, and nuzzled his neck.

In a restless mood, she didn't attempt to work. With Billy in the stroller, she ambled over to Adele's. She needed company, another voice other than the one in her head that had kept letting thoughts of Alex intrude all day.

Rubbing the ache at the back of her neck, she stood at Adele's door and listened to the chimes of the doorbell. Carly knew the woman was home. Her car was in the driveway. So why wasn't she answering? She pushed the doorbell again. This time, the door squeaked open to a slit.

"Oh, thank goodness." Her eyes peering past Carly, Adele eased the door open farther, then whisked Carly into her house. "Do you see him?"

Confused, Carly balked just inside the front door. "See who?"

Panic in her eyes, Adele scurried to the window. "Look," she insisted, bending down a slat in the blinds to peer outside.

Carly peeked out the opening. "What am I looking for?"

"I called Dora, but she wasn't home. Oh, I'm so glad you came by. What should I do about him?"

Carly drew away from the blinds. "Adele, I don't understand."

Again she bent back the slat. "See the car. The dark one across the street."

Carly eyed the black sedan and the man sitting behind the steering wheel, his gaze riveted on Adele's house.

"He's been there for hours. Just sits there. He knows I can't call the police for that. They would think I was a silly old lady."

Carly swung around. "Is he—Vestor?" she asked, recalling the name Adele had previously mentioned.

With her nod, tears glimmered in the woman's eyes.

Anger for her blossomed in Carly. "Here." She held Billy out to Adele. "Take Billy."

"What are you going to do?"

"Find out what he wants," she declared while storming toward the door.

"You be careful."

"I will be." Closing the door behind her, Carly straightened her back. No one had a right to terrorize anymore. When she was within a few feet of the car, the man's menacing stare chilled her. She kept walking toward him until he revved the engine. Uncertain what he planned to do, Carly froze in place. A standoff ensued. Their eyes met, his narrowed and ominous, hers steady and challenging.

She took only another step. Veering the car away from the curb, he zipped it toward her. Only a jump back prevented it from hitting her. Stunned, her heart banging against the wall of her chest, she squinted after the car, zeroing in on the license-plate number.

Adele had been right about the police. Carly's phone call to them proved futile. Disgusted, she slumped back on a chair as the detective, in what she supposed was his most compassionate tone, expounded on the need for proof.

"Without it, all you have is a suspicious-looking character in a parked car."

"What about his harassment? She's an elderly woman. He's scaring the daylights out of her."

"Got any proof?"

That word again.

"If you get proof or..." He paused as if hesitant. "Or if he does something to her, call us."

Carly clenched her teeth and set down the receiver.

"You tried," Adele said sympathetically.

Who was supposed to be consoling whom? Guilt descended on Carly for not trying harder to get through the detective's thick skull.

This was not one of her best days, she decided when she entered the house later. In less than a few hours, she'd been spooked by a hoodlum, frustrated by police response to what she viewed as a threat and was still disturbed about leaving Adele alone.

Restless and uneasy, Carly paced the living room. While she didn't need to lean on anyone, she would have liked to hear a familiar voice. Briefly, she glanced at the telephone. How would her family react to a simple hello? All she needed to do was tell her aunt she was back in the Bay Area.

No! What would be the point in calling her aunt? She hadn't left her on good terms. Before she'd gone out the door, her aunt's disapproval had hung in the air between them. She assumed her aunt had viewed her strike for freedom as a personal affront. But she hadn't been thumbing her nose at her aunt's life-style, at all she'd given Carly. She'd simply needed freedom from the endless expectations of what was proper and acceptable. She decided there would be no purpose in calling, no words to bridge the anger between them.

Carrying Billy up the stairs for a diaper change, in passing, she snatched up the portable phone. She knew exactly who would calm her if she called.

Billy's gibberish wafted on the air while she slipped a clean diaper under his bottom. "Yes, I'll call Auntie Renee," she said lightly, pretending communication with him while she was wiggling his arms into a long-sleeved shirt.

As his head popped through the shirt opening, he bubbled a sound that resembled the putt-putt of a propeller engine.

Carly went on with her conversation. "She'll give me one of her I-told-you-so lectures."

While Carly pulled a pair of bib overalls over his small body, he gurgled a succession of G's.

"You're right. I am in trouble." She kissed him and reached for the telephone. She managed to tug socks on his constantly moving feet before Renee answered.

"I thought you would never call," her friend practically yelled in her ear. "I've got news. I met someone."

Carly matched Renee's exuberant tone. "Who? Where?"

"At work. He's a musician." Renee rambled on about her latest love's looks. "A real deep-thinker type. He likes to talk about the meaning behind music, though half the time I'm not sure what he's saying."

It was so settling to hear the familiar sound of Renee's rapid speech.

"So tell me everything that's happened to you," Renee said.

Carly pushed a shoe onto Billy's foot. "There isn't much to tell," she said and laughed silently as Billy sent the untied shoe flying in the air. With a quick lean to the side, she caught it.

Exasperation entered Renee's voice. "That means plenty has happened."

Again, Carly nudged the shoe onto Billy's foot and quickly tied the laces. "Things are getting, well, when he's around, I feel—" She concentrated on completing the task on Billy's second foot. How could she explain what she couldn't identify?

"That's called lust, kiddo."

"No, I've known that before." It was more than desire. Though she didn't always see eye-to-eye with Alex, she liked being with him. She enjoyed the sound of his voice, the sight of his smile, the tenderness he gave so freely to her and Billy. "This is something else."

"Careful. You might be confusing your feelings for Billy with feelings for him because he's the father."

"That musician is having a definite effect on you," Carly teased while tying the laces on Billy's second shoe.

"I told you. We spend hours discussing the mysteries of life." The humor in Renee's tone gave way to one filled with concern. "But the big question for you is obvious. Are you falling in love with Alex?"

God, was she? Could she have felt so much so quickly for a man she didn't care deeply about? And if she accepted what she felt for him, at what moment would the happiness she wanted to grab hold of come crashing down on her because she'd acted rashly or failed him in some way?

She ended her conversation with Renee and after asking Dora to check on Billy in his playpen, Carly ambled outside to her workshop. Maybe Renee was right. What if this was merely a physical attraction?

What if it wasn't?

Nerves on edge from her own thoughts, she settled at her potter's wheel. Instantly, as she let her hands move down the clay, her whole body relaxed. It was always like this when she worked. Carly believed that if people would just buy a mound of clay and play with it, every psychiatrist and therapist in the world would go out of business.

By late afternoon, fatigue began settling in. Surveying what she'd accomplished so far, Carly acknowledged a mixture of satisfaction and frustration. She could have done more, but more than once, she'd stopped because of the heat in the shed.

She took a break to prepare a bottle for Billy, then relaxed with him in the shade of some nearby trees for nearly an hour. No time was wasted, she told herself. She murmured soft words to him while he amused himself with a ball that jingled. All the while, Carly mentally created her next piece. Before she put Billy down for his nap, she'd already decided on four different designs.

But she still didn't know what to do about Alex. Love didn't conquer all. The problem between them would appear in time. As much as he needed order in his life, she would surely disrupt it. Yet, when he touched her, kissed her, her blood pounded. And wise or not, she wanted everything with him.

Alex labored through a meeting with quality control about production. The moment he returned to his office, he touched the seashell pottery. He needed some link with Carly. More and more, he needed that. Nothing was as simple as it was supposed to be. The marriage in name only had been complicated by emotion right from the start. He'd been giving her space, and all the while, he was aching for her. Nothing helped, not even work.

If he thought she didn't care, he would have blocked his own need, but he'd seen passion in her eyes, had felt it in her kiss. And his patience was stretched to the limit.

He wasn't getting anything done. Annoyed with the time he was wasting, he left work early. Though his briefcase bulged with reports to analyze, instead of going straight to his study, Alex climbed the stairs to the nursery. With a child's soft snore, his son slept. Smiling, Alex yanked off his tie and wandered to his room to change. By the time he'd zipped up his jeans and pulled a polo shirt over his head, he was frowning again.

He'd identified the problem. The quiet was unnerving. Where was she? Why didn't he hear Carly humming or the sound of her soft laugh from the kitchen while she passed time with Dora?

A few minutes of wandering the house left Alex more puzzled and disturbed. The mere thought of Carly not being here rustled an empty feeling within him. It stunned him. He'd never needed anyone that much. *Need.* Wanting a woman was one thing, but need meant so much more.

With another walk through the house, Alex stopped at Dora's door. Inside her room, she was packing for her trip to her sister's. "Is Carly home?"

"She's in the garden shed," she said while folding a sweater.

"What's she doing there?"

"Find out for yourself." She plopped her rump on top of the bulging suitcase to close it.

Alex caught her sly grin before he left her room. He didn't feel lighthearted enough to verbally spar with her.

Puzzled, he crossed the yard and descended the hill. From several feet away, he heard the sound of Carly singing along with an upbeat tune that was blaring from the radio.

He found her sitting in the small windowless shed, her back bent, her head bowed, her nose aimed over the center of a potter's wheel. Adeptly, her palms squeezed a glob of clay, then slowly coaxed the walls of the resultant cylinder upward slowly.

Beneath her hands, the clay miraculously took shape, her delicate fingers smoothing over the wet mass until the beauty of a vase became apparent.

A bead of sweat on his forehead, Alex brushed it away with the back of his hand. The air in the room was hot and sultry, reminding him of a stormy summer night when he'd been in Florida.

Quiet, he scanned shelves filled with vases and pots, shallow and deep bowls and one that resembled a tureen. On the bottom shelf was a teapot with several cups, all decorated in a soft gray-white with a blue-flowered decoration.

As the wheel stopped humming, he ended his study of an Oriental-looking lamp. In the slow, lazy motion of a cat, she straightened her back and stretched.

Before she noticed him, he backed away.

The chill of a late-afternoon breeze alerted Carly to the time. Stopping for the day, she cleaned her work area then hurried into the house to get Billy's bottle ready.

With it warmed, she went up the stairs, but she braked at the doorway of the nursery.

Sitting cross-legged on the floor, Alex was rocking his son and soothing him with what sounded like a rap version of "Casey at the Bat."

"That's the best I can do," he murmured, grateful that the baby was too young to critique the few lines he'd improvised.

His eyes wide with curiosity, Billy tipped his head, then his bottom lip trembled with the threat of more tears.

"Oh, don't do that. Come on. Don't do that." Alex patted his son's back.

Touched by the gentle scene, Carly felt all opposition withering away. Here was the man who could make her believe in everything she'd imagined—and in them.

"If only you could talk," Alex said on a laugh to his son.

Now that the performance had ended, Carly entered the room. "He is. He's hungry."

Alex sprang to his feet with the balance a gymnast would have envied.

Taking Billy from him, her eyes locked with his. He could sweep her away with one of those looks. It warmed her blood, kindled the fire within her. How often could this happen? she wondered breathlessly.

Alex didn't step back. He cupped a hand behind her neck but kept the pressure gentle. He wanted nothing more at the moment than to feel some semblance of closeness with her.

"Dora's almost ready to leave," she told him.

As she set Billy against her shoulder to rock him slowly, Alex tore his gaze from her lips. He wanted to hold her. Just hold her. Sure, he wanted her with such consuming desire, he thought he'd go mad from it. But there was that need again to feel as if they were a part of each other even when they weren't touching. "I'm driving her to the airport," he said.

Fighting the fire inside her, Carly simply nodded, but a realization swarmed in on her.

They would be alone.

A crescent moon slipped behind the clouds. With darkness mantling the house, Alex returned home. He'd waited with Dora at the airport, bought her a drink before her flight to Maine. After the plane had taken off, he'd found an all-night coffee shop and had consumed three cups before heading home.

Without turning on any lights, he climbed the stairs.

Half an hour later, he gave up any pretense of going to sleep, crawled out of bed and yanked up his jeans. Barefoot, he shuffled downstairs to the kitchen.

She stood near the open refrigerator door, cast in an ethereal glow, her hair pale, her face partially hidden by shadow. Her silhouette was vague but enticing beneath the thin cottony cloth of an oversize nightshirt.

It was a creak, nothing more that made Carly look over her shoulder. The sight of him bare-chested reminded her just how alive and needy she was. She couldn't stop herself from taking a lengthy view of him. Corded muscles rippled with a simple movement as if inviting her touch. "Want a midnight snack?"

"No, just coffee." Standing by the coffeemaker now, Alex cast a frustrated glance over his shoulder. Wearing a wide-necked, pale blue nightshirt with buttons down the front and her hair tousled, she looked young, sleepy-eyed. She looked beautiful. Downright irresistible.

His mind full of her, he gripped the cup of coffee he'd poured and eyed the concoction she'd prepared, a blend of raspberries, peaches, bananas and what looked like crumbled graham crackers. As she pivoted away from the sink, the cottony fabric of her nightshirt molded to the underside of her breasts. Before his mind totally shut down, he looked back down at the steaming brew in his cup. "You're going to have nightmares eating like that so late at night."

"Dreams." Carly licked the spoon. "I always dream after eating this."

For the first time in a long while, Alex had been doing his share of fantasizing. Why, of all the women in the world, was she so alluring and irresistible to him? "Dream about what?" he asked, stepping behind her and brushing hair from the nape of her neck.

Her voice softened as his mouth suddenly grazed her skin. "I don't remember, but I always feel good in the morning."

Alex felt her shiver and thought her answer ironic. If she rushed away again, she would be feeling rested and happy after eating what would deliver dismal results to anyone who didn't have a cast-iron stomach. And him? She would haunt his dreams. "Do you still want to open your shop?"

Excitement always spiraled through her when Carly considered the possibility, but she could barely think at the moment. "I need to sell more pottery first and save more money and—" She stilled as he caressed her shoulder and turned her to face him.

Alex felt none of the tenseness she usually exhibited when he was so near. "You can afford to do it now. You're my wife." His mouth moved to her cheek. "You can have anything you want."

Soft. Compelling. His voice swirled around her like a warm caress. As his mouth warmed her collarbone, she braced herself for more sensations, but too many swarmed in on her.

With her softness so near, the craving slammed at him. He needed to lose himself in her. He needed the heat. "Anything," he whispered against the corner of her mouth.

Him. She wanted him. She had no thoughts beyond him as a seductive tenderness weaved around them. Her pulse thudding, she framed his face with her hands.

Alex laughed as much with relief as humor. "You're driving me crazy," he admitted. "I can't think about anything except you."

She couldn't catch her breath. It seemed only his kiss would keep her alive. She fell into his arms, her mouth already on his. Every time he'd held her, it had felt so right. She'd wanted his embrace, his kisses. Now, with his lips savoring hers, desire hummed through her. She glided her hands up the smooth muscular planes of his chest. He felt wonderful. He tasted wonderful. Dark, wild, mysterious. All she'd remembered, all she'd imagined.

She'd never understood the special, almost mystical feeling promised in love songs. But faint, it whispered on the air to her now. Taste commanded her. Seduction kindled a warm pleasure within her. Persuasion invaded her heart.

Her eyes fluttering, she gripped his bare shoulders. It was a moment to explore, to discover, to seek what was still fresh and unknown even as it became more familiar. Always she yearned for what promised a new adventure. This went beyond that.

She gave completely. Beyond the desire, she sensed the specialness of this man. There was no turning back. While the power of desire taunted her, it was a helplessness she couldn't deny or explain that made her desperate for him. Breathless, as he lifted his mouth from hers, she stared into eyes hooded with the heat of passion and the cloudiness of confusion. Like him, she knew the craving was too powerful to resist. And like him, she was perplexed about what would follow. She only knew at this moment that the ground wasn't firm beneath her feet, and this time they couldn't pretend the kiss had been a mistake. Definitely, it hadn't been a mistake.

"Tell me what you want," he said in a voice huskier than usual.

"I want you." Her own words echoing in her head, she clung with the same intensity as her lips answered his. But he controlled the moment, his mouth taking, his tongue arousing. She heard a moan, knew it was her own and yanked at the snap on his jeans. Need sped through her. Raw and potent, it urged her fingers to his zipper. Heat rose within her even as she felt her nightshirt slither down and coolness caress her bare flesh.

So much was left unsaid. So much was ignored. But only his kiss, his touch, their need mattered. An intimacy she'd never expected with him bound her to him.

Tilting her head back, she gave his lips freedom to explore her throat.

Then he lifted her into his arms. She couldn't speak. She could only take in the reality of a moment she'd thought a part of a dream as he carried her up the stairs, as his mouth moved over her face and throat until she was breathless from his kisses.

With a hunger that thrilled Carly, his lips fastened on hers again. She seemed to float down to the mattress. Breaths blended. Tongues met and challenged. Her heart pounding, she shifted beneath him, and together, they tugged his jeans from him.

Her own needs alive, she slid her hands over his bare back, marveling at the hard contours, the tautness of his body, the warmth of him beneath her hands. Needing, she grazed the muscular flesh of his hip. She closed her eyes, letting her fingertips dance across his skin like a blind person's. All that mattered at the moment was to touch what was still a mystery. Splaying her fingers down his stomach, she felt him quiver. Power rushed heat through her.

But he took command with a fluttering caress of his lips or a seductive stroke of his tongue. He sought one breast and then the other. He savored, arousing each nipple, then taunted her belly. Through a cloud of sensation, she felt his hardness, but he held back.

Pleasure hurled her into a whirlwind of ecstasy. If anything existed beyond them, she wasn't aware of it. She was floating. And there was only him and the lingering heat of his mouth, only the touch of his hand seeking the moistness between her thighs.

She arched against his hand, pressing her head into the pillow as the warmth of his breath seared her. Persuading, arousing, his mouth claimed her, his tongue branded her. An awakening raced over her. All at once, she knew love. She'd admitted the possibility before. Now she accepted it without reservation.

He urged her on, his moist tongue overpowering even the hint of a rational thought. With abandon, she gave in to the sensations that weakened as they pleasured her. Beneath his slightest whisper of a caress, her skin heated. Urgency spiraled into madness. He made her crave, he made her ache, yet she felt from him only tenderness, undeniable sweetness, as if he'd found a treasure to marvel over.

On a plea, she called his name, wanting to rest and catch her breath. And she wanted none of that, nothing except him.

At her shudder against him, his hands sought her arching hips, and he raised above her. Carly wrapped her legs around him in invitation, and as he pressed down and entered her, a mindlessness grabbed hold. Perfectly, they fit together, their flesh bathing in a sultry heat. While his raspy breath mingled with hers, their bodies moved as one.

All slowness, all tenderness gone, she arched to draw him deeper. Relentless, his body took her with him until only the enticing friction of his flesh against and in her and the fury of need rushing over them existed.

"Now," she heard herself cry. "Please, now."

Whatever might come later suddenly didn't matter.

Chapter Eleven

A streak of sunlight pierced the room. Alex forced his eyes open but didn't move, aware of the warmth of Carly beside him. She curled even closer, nestling her head on his chest and draping her arm across his midsection. He'd been so certain that he needed only once with her to curb what had begun to seem like an obsession, but the night of loving only made him want her more.

When he shifted, she migrated to the space he'd vacated as if seeking the warmth where he'd been. She murmured something unintelligible, and he found himself wishing it was his name. To dissect why he felt that way required more strength than he was capable of at the moment.

Raking a hand through tousled hair, he eased himself from Carly, then picked up the telephone receiver.

As if an alien had taken over his body, he punched out the number for his office and did the unthinkable.

"Webb Electronics Corporation, Mr. Kane's office."

Alex shot another look at Carly. "Ginnie, I won't be in today," he told his secretary.

"Yes, sir."

Alex heard curiosity in her voice. During the seven years she'd worked for him, he'd never taken a day off except to search for his son.

She murmured another polite response before he ended the call.

With a laugh at himself, Alex found himself doing something else he hadn't done since the first day of summer vacation when he was eight; he went back to bed.

As he slid his arm under Carly's head, she sleepily murmured something he couldn't decipher.

"Go back to sleep," he urged softly, tugging her closer. Some part of him that seemed new and unfamiliar craved more quiet moments of just holding her.

Feather-light, she kissed his shoulder, then in a natural and unselfconscious move, she snuggled, draping a slender leg over his, and pressed her soft, womanly contours against him. For the first time in his life, he had no idea where he was going. And he didn't care, he realized as she tipped back her head. With the lazy shift of her body, with a simple caress of her soft hands, she made his head swim. His gaze clinging to her face, he laced his fingers with hers and lowered his head to the softness of her breast. Right now, all he wanted was to please her.

* * *

When Alex awoke later, he was alone. He couldn't say how long he'd slept, but sunlight poured into the room. Tossing back the covers, he pushed himself to the edge of the mattress.

Fifteen minutes later, he was showered and dressed. Carly. She'd been his first thought upon awakening. Never had he received so much from a woman nor been asked to give so much. She'd forced him to rethink his plans, to do the unexpected. He'd become more involved with her than he'd ever anticipated. He'd made promises when he'd married her and wasn't sure they wouldn't eventually be broken. Yet, somehow, he would try his damnedest not to hurt her. She'd become too important, too special to him for him to break that vow.

He followed the sound of the radio to the kitchen. She stood in the soft glow of morning sunlight. Without doing anything, she enticed him, made him yearn to hold her. Alex stepped close behind her and touched her hair, pushing it back so he could nibble her ear. "Where were you?"

Yearning for just this, the feel of his arms around her again. She'd been muddling her way through too many conflicting emotions, and one caress from him, possessive and steady, skimming her thigh, was all she'd needed to know that last night hadn't been a mistake— or a dream. But where did they go from here? Suddenly, she wanted so much. On a sigh, she swayed back to rest her head on his shoulder. "Thinking about you."

"Amazing." He smiled against her cheek. "We agree on something."

"We do?" Following the urge of his hand at her waist, Carly faced him. "What's that?"

"I was thinking about you, too." Alex kissed the bridge of her nose. "I was thinking how beautiful you are. How often you make me smile," he whispered, his breath hot against her cheek. "How much I want you," he murmured softly.

Late-morning sunlight flooded the rooms before they settled on the wrought-iron chairs on the terrace outside his bedroom. "I wasn't sure what you would like for breakfast." Carly looked up from pouring coffee for each of them and smiled at the lazy contented look on his face. "Adele made these," she said, lifting a linen napkin to reveal a basket of cinnamon rolls.

Feeling mellow, Alex had to prod himself to lean forward for his coffee cup. "Did you want to invite her to the party?"

She'd done that days ago. If possible, she would have invited the mail carrier and everyone else she knew so she would be surrounded by familiar faces. "I invited her," she finally answered.

Alex caught the concern in her eyes. "Are you worried about the party because Dora's gone?"

Worried was a mild description. Her stomach clenched every time she thought about the evening with his business associates and friends.

Wanting to offer reassurance, Alex took her hand. "You don't need to be concerned. You did a terrific job when Doug and Julia were here. And the caterer we contacted knows what she's doing. All you have to do is be boss lady for the day."

Because she sensed he wanted to see it, Carly smiled. "I'll stay out of the rain that night."

Alex hunched forward. Cupping her chin in his hand, he tipped her face up to him. A soft longing stirred inside him to ease away the troubled line marring her forehead. "You don't have anything to prove to me, Carly."

Maybe to herself. That eventful evening of her engagement party she'd made a wrong decision, and disaster had followed. She desperately didn't want history to repeat itself.

"Do you believe me?" he asked, wishing by touch he could make her smile.

With the stroke of his thumb at the corner of her lips, her skin tingled. "You're very persuasive."

The need to see the light back in her eyes overwhelmed him. "Good. Because the only thing I have doubts about is whether I'm going to be able to finish one of these," he said, slanting a look at the oversize rolls.

Eagerly, Carly grasped his efforts to lighten the mood. "Humongous, aren't they? Adele said that's the way they make them in Texas."

From the terrace outside his bedroom, the gables of Adele's Victorian house peeked through the trees between their properties. Alex considered what Dora had told him previously about the elderly woman's problem. A man in his position couldn't afford to be linked with anything criminal, even as a good Samaritan. "Do you see her often?"

"I check on her every day."

Cautiously, he sipped his coffee. "Carly, tell her to call the police if she's having trouble. The sight of them will probably stop the guy. It's their job, not yours. You're my wife now and—" He caught himself from saying more. Wasn't this exactly the concern she'd been dealing with just minutes ago?

A butter knife in her hand, Carly frowned at him. She'd been right. He did have expectations she would have trouble accepting.

Alex damned himself for causing the flicker of uneasiness he saw again in her eyes. He sensed they would have more words, some angry, about the subject of Adele Bridelman's trouble. For the moment, he kept himself from saying more.

But later, while he drove them into San Francisco, he wondered how to make sense about it to someone with such a gentle soul.

As he'd done during the whole trip, Billy continued to vocalize while Carly pushed the back seat forward to unsnap him from his car seat. Carly nuzzled his neck. "You are a chatterbox." Slinging the diaper bag over her shoulder, she scanned their surroundings. The bell-clanging of a cable car widened Billy's eyes. "*We* want to ride in one of those. Don't we, Billy?" She leaned close to kiss his cheek and received what sounded like an agreeable laughing gurgle.

Alex frowned at the hordes climbing into the cable car. "It's crowded."

Carly cracked a smile at a typical Alex observation and linked her hand in his. "We can squeeze on."

Along with dozens of tourists, they inched their way onto the cable car. Reaching around her, Alex clung to a strap. More people climbed in, pressing him closer to her. The collapsed stroller in one hand, Alex ignored a push from behind by a stranger. Being crowded wasn't so bad, he decided, as jammed against Carly, he felt all the feminine contours of her body.

In her arms, Billy gleefully babbled at other passengers. One of them oohed over the vista of San Francisco Bay and Alcatraz Island.

Alex angled his head to peer around Carly, but the sight before him didn't seem important. Discreetly, he sought the softness at the slender curve of her neck.

In response, Carly squinched her neck. "Can you see the view?"

"I'm enjoying it."

Carly laughed. "What are you doing?"

"By your giggle, a poor job of romancing you," he murmured.

She swayed back against him as the cable car jerked down the hill. "Romancing?"

He pressed his lips to her temple. "About time, isn't it?"

Since she'd never expected it, she wasn't sure what to say.

"You look cute with your mouth hanging open."

Carly shut it quickly and playfully elbowed him.

When the car stopped, they made their way off with the others. Bending over to set Billy in his stroller, Alex looked up and saw her staring up at a sky that was darkening to a deep gray with the promise of rain. A long time had passed since he'd allowed himself the time to relax, but she was drawing him along with her. Through her eyes, everything seemed more interesting, from the horse-drawn carriages to the freighters and expensive yachts floating by in the bay. Yet, none of that was new to her, either, he realized. "Did you always live at your aunt's when you were here before?"

Carly ended her preoccupation with a sea gull's flight. "Yep. Right on Nob Hill."

And she'd left it, she'd run from it, Alex reminded himself. Had it been a rebellious act that had made her flee to the apartment of that artist? Though he considered the past unimportant, he couldn't curb his curiosity about the man. Her engagement with Westerly hadn't been the love match of the century. But what had her feelings been for the artist? Had she loved him? "Was there ever anyone besides Westerly?"

Carly slitted her eyes to look down at him. "Kind of late to wonder, isn't it?"

Standing, Alex slid his sunglasses on. "Just curious. Once before, I asked you if there was someone in your life who would object to your living with me. You said no," he went on because suddenly he needed to know. "But was there?"

"If there had been, I would never have come with you."

He ignored her amused tone. "Why wasn't there someone?"

"Why should there have been?"

How could there not have been? Alex wondered. He couldn't be the only man whose knees she weakened when she smiled. "You're a lovely woman."

She met his stare with a wry smile. "Alex, what is this about?"

His eyebrows knitted. It was about jealousy. It was about a need to know if someone had won her heart. "I wondered if there was any man you'd ever lived with."

"Was there ever any woman that you—"

"No." He caught the amusement in her eyes. "Just answer me. Okay?"

"Okay." She laughed and laced her fingers with his. "Living with someone and being in love with him aren't the same, are they?"

He leaned close, leveling one of those unflinching stares that was meant to intimidate. "Who did you live with?"

Carly laughed. "I lived with another potter for a while."

"But you weren't in love with him?"

"I loved him." A gentle breeze whipping around them, Carly pushed back hair blown forward across her eyes. "But I wasn't in love with him," she said and wheeled Billy's stroller toward the icy carts on the sidewalk where vendors dispensed seafood. "Let's buy something there."

"The man?"

Carly grinned, deciding he looked incredibly sexy when jealous. "He was wonderful. Talented."

Alex wished he hadn't asked. "You weren't in love with him, but you slept with him?"

"Who said that?"

Alex frowned. Why was this conversation becoming so difficult? "You didn't sleep with him?" he asked.

Carly sent him a breezy smile. "Of course not."

How could a man live with her and not want her? He'd had a devil of a time with that dilemma.

"He taught me so much about pottery," Carly informed him.

That made sense to him. "So he was a mentor?"

Carly understood now why he'd been so successful. Tenacity made him weather every door slammed in his face. "I thought of him as more," she said in answer to his question. Deliberately, she slid his sunglasses to the bridge of his nose so she could see his eyes. "Like a grandfather."

"Grandfather?"

"He was seventy-eight years old."

"He was—"

He looked so dumbfounded that she couldn't help giggling. "Yes. When his brother became ill, he needed my room so I left."

Alex wavered between amusement and exasperation as her eyes mocked him. He supposed he deserved that verbal runaround. With anyone else, he would have been infuriated. With her, he wanted to laugh. "Did you enjoy having fun at my expense?"

Her smile flashed at him. "Immensely." Carly darted a look around for an available table. "I'll grab that," she said, certain he would balk at walking while they ate crab legs.

Around them, children laughed, young couples strolled, tourists aimed cameras. In his stroller, Billy jabbered with delight at the strange sights and the unusual scents drifting out from the various shops.

Late-afternoon sunlight shimmered on the water, reminding Alex as he set crab legs before her that he would pay big time for playing hooky from the office and the mound of paperwork on his desk.

"Don't think about business," Carly said, guessing by his brief frown that his mind had wandered.

"I didn't know one of your talents was mind reading."

With exuberance, she cracked a crab leg. "All type A people slip back a notch occasionally."

Humor danced in his eyes. "Can I think about your business?"

"Mine?" Her hands stilled. "What about mine?"

"There are some artists' shops you might like to see. Next time we're here, we can go there."

"Oh, I've visited them already. I needed to find someone who would let me use his kiln."

Leaning back in the chair, Alex chewed slowly. "Why don't you have a kiln?"

She grinned. "It's not like going out and buying a toaster."

His fingers wet from tugging the crabmeat from the leg, Alex snatched up a napkin. "Well, if you want—" He didn't finish his sentence, but followed Carly's stare to the tall white-haired man approaching them.

Bennett Doleman was no stranger to Carly. When she and his daughter had been scooting around their boarding-school auditorium lugging musical instruments, he'd offered words of praise about the concert in which they'd just performed.

"Bennett Doleman is chairman of the board for Webb Electronics," he told her.

Full circle, Carly mused. Ironically, Alex had drawn her back to a world she'd left—no, ran from. "Do you want me to grab a napkin and pretend I'm busing the table?" she asked lightly.

Alex gave her a pseudo scowl. "Just keep your cute bottom on that chair."

"My cute—"

"Just stay," he practically growled, aware as she was of what he'd said. Peripherally, he caught her quiet giggle before Doleman reached their table.

"Carly." Doleman took her hand in his. "How nice it was to hear about your marriage to Alex."

"Thank you." Carly delivered a smile for a man she'd truly liked. "We're happy you're pleased."

Alex restrained a grin. Leave it to Carly to subtly remind Doleman he'd instigated their marriage.

"You're looking well, Mr. Doleman."

Doleman's eyes twinkled with amusement. "Now, I believe I was supposed to say that to you. You look quite lovely."

Manners drilled into her provided an ease for small talk with him. "How is Deborah?" Carly asked about her old school chum.

"My daughter lives in Hyannis Port now. She would love to hear from you, I'm sure. I'll remember to give her telephone number to Alex." His pale eyes strayed to Billy. "A handsome boy."

Content, Billy gurgled at the attention and shook the giant plastic ring in his hand, taking delight in its rattling sound.

"It's been quite some time since I've seen your aunt. How is she?"

Alex shifted his gaze to Carly. With an unmistakable tenseness, she curled fingers tightly around her napkin. Were memories crowding her mind? he wondered. He could do little about that, but he could ease some of the discomfort Doleman's question was causing. "We've been busy and haven't had a chance to see her yet."

Seeming to accept the excuse, Doleman nodded and smiled. "When you do, say hello to her for me," he instructed, then swiveled a look back at his table. "No doubt Leone has noticed I'm missing. We were at the political speech for Cortland. I'll tell you about it tomorrow."

Alex shifted his gaze away from Doleman joining an inquisitive-looking Leone Pipperton and saw Carly's frown. Share it with me, he wanted to say.

"Are you done?" Carly asked.

Whether he was or not, she'd already bounded to a stand. Alex kept silent until they'd strolled away from the crowd. "Do you want to see her?"

Carly shook her head. "There would be no reason to. We didn't part amiably." She offered him a semblance of a smile. "Can I buy you an ice cream?"

For the moment, Alex went along with her efforts to lighten the mood. "Do you know how much you've eaten?"

"And with good reason."

Puzzlement slipped into his voice. "Reason?"

"Yes. See how little you know about me. I can be quite logical when it's necessary." She paid for a double scoop of Rocky Road, then faced him. "I know something you don't remember."

Standing near, he placed his hand lightly at the curve of her waist. "What's that?"

Carly swayed closer to offer him a lick of ice cream from her cone. "Dora's not home."

With a swipe at the ice cream, his tongue savored the flavor of creamy chocolate.

"Which means one of us will have to make dinner."

"Ah, now I get it." Smiling, he brushed at ice cream on a corner of her mouth. "You don't expect to get any."

She sent him a feigned affronted look. "I cook, or have you forgotten my culinary masterpiece?"

Actually, her quickly put-together dinner for Doug and Julie had been delicious, though different. "Okay, but not something weird."

Playfully, Carly punched him. "Oh, ye of little faith. I have a delicious recipe for peanut butter soup."

They ate chili and crackers at the kitchen table.

As Alex fanned his mouth, Carly laughed. "Too hot for you?"

His mouth was on fire. "No, it's not too hot for me," he said, refusing to admit the truth when she was spooning chili into her mouth nonstop.

"I forgot to tell you." Carly waited for him to finish draining half a glass of water. "We have new neighbors. The real estate company's sign came down yesterday. He said that the buyers are a young couple with a son—older than Billy. About nine or ten."

Alex noted the brightness that had flared in her eyes. She was eager to make new friends. That wouldn't be difficult. She had a tendency to talk to everyone she met.

"Would you want to?" Carly repeated.

"Want to?"

Carly laughed. "Welcome them."

"Whatever you want," he said so easily he shocked himself. All his life, he'd only cared about what he wanted. It hadn't been selfishness motivating him; he'd had no one else to consider—until now, until her.

Gathering their dishes, Carly nudged him with her hip. "Want to play gin rummy?" Her words ended on a giggle as he caught her at the waist and tugged her down to his lap.

"I'll warn you now." His breath fanned her ear. "I always win."

Carly loved his smile, loved when he offered a rarely seen lighter side. "We'll see."

Confident, Alex joined her in the dining room. In his youth, he'd been a master at all card games, enough of one to win food money when he'd been financially scraping the bottom. But after a while, he knew he'd met his match. Every hand, she beat him.

Not bothering to hide her grin, Carly left him scowling and recalculating the scores and climbed the stairs for bed. "See you upstairs."

"Did you cheat?" he asked, taking the steps two at a time to follow her.

On her knees, she was retrieving a slipper from under the bed.

"Did you?"

"Don't be a sore loser."

"I'm not a sore loser," he murmured, whipping his shirt over his head.

"You're going to set a terrible example for Billy," she sang out.

Flinging the shirt aside, Alex stepped up behind her. "Terrible."

Carly turned in his embrace and backed up toward the bed. On a quick, short laugh, she fell onto the mattress, dragging him down with her. "You don't sound upset."

"I am." His mouth at her throat, he tugged at the snap on her jeans. "I'm very upset that you're still dressed."

A giggle flowed up from her throat.

"But not for long," he whispered as she raised her hips and aided him in pulling down her jeans.

Laughing, Carly rolled with him, using her foot to push the tight denim off one of her legs. "I'm still not undressed."

With her stocking feet curled around his leg, Alex's chuckle rippled in the silent air. "You make me senseless."

Teasingly, she stroked his bare belly. "Because I'm so irresistible?"

Tantalizing. Alluring. Enticing. Alex nearly closed his eyes. "Guess so."

"Such flattery will make me weak..." Her voice trailed off as his lips silenced her. Then, she was lost, his taste clouding her mind.

Chapter Twelve

Her chin propped on her hand, Carly stared down at Alex and outlined the smile curving his lips. She'd found passion and companionship with him. And suddenly it wasn't enough. She wanted more—she wanted his love. "Good morning," she said on a sigh.

With effort, Alex forced his eyes open. Tousled from the action of his hands, her hair wildly framed her face. He inched closer to her body, to its comforting warmth. Fantasy. He'd never believed in wasting time on it. Was that all they were sharing? Or was this the good time in a marriage? For this kind of happiness, he thought people would hold on, stand together through any kind of trouble.

An unexpected wave of contentment swept through him. He didn't want to think beyond it. To do so meant trying to understand his need to be with her. Posses-

sively, he threaded his fingers through her hair and began to draw her face to his. A thumping that sounded
like the persistent beat of a tom-tom stilled him.
" 'Morning."

"Not convincing." Carly traced the frown line between his eyebrows. "Let's try that again," she said,
then pressed her lips to his, hard.

Alex smiled and slid a hand down to her bare backside. "That's some good morning."

"Uh-huh. Does it give you any ideas?" she murmured against the side of his neck.

The stroke of her hand made him grab a quick
breath. "You—" The thumping began again. "What is
that noise?" It was impossible to ignore. Certain now
that it was coming from the nursery, in a swift move, he
swung his legs out of bed.

Lazily, Carly stretched and took her fill of his sleek,
muscular body. "I like looking at you."

A step from the door, Alex swung a grin back at her.
"That was my line."

Carly laughed and stretched again, then shoved the
sheet away with her legs. Breathing deeply, she nudged
herself out of bed. The idea of passing through Billy's
room in her birthday suit halted her a foot from the bed.
With a quick scan of the room, she snatched Alex's
shirt, and while slipping it on, she crossed into the
nursery.

Beside the crib, Alex draped an arm over the railing.
Lifting his head, Billy rocked back and forth on his
tummy for a few seconds, then rolled onto his back and
banged his feet with a steady beat any drummer would
envy.

A thread of pride tightened around Alex's chest. Sometimes while looking at his son, he felt total disbelief that he'd been a part in making him. He'd accepted sex as an enjoyable part of life, but he'd always been too responsible not to consider the consequences. One time, just one, after enormous career successes for Amanda and him, they'd gotten carried away by a celebratory mood. He hadn't thought beyond that moment. After all, other people had children, not him. Rug rats, he'd thought back then.

With a gentle stroke, Alex brushed wispy strands of dark hair from Billy's forehead and received a smile from his son. There had been no way for him to know how much emotion one little smile from someone so small would arouse within him.

At the touch of Carly's hand on his shoulder, Alex looked up. "What's this?" he asked and fingered a button on the shirt she was wearing.

"I heard your stomach rumble. I thought you might want breakfast."

"That was your stomach," he teased back while he deftly opened the top button. Beneath his knuckles, he felt her heartbeat quicken. "How hungry are you?"

The softness in his tone stirred her smile. How was it possible to feel so much excitement when he was barely touching her? "Starving."

Enthusiastic as ever, when Carly cooked she used every inch of counter space. At the kitchen doorway, Alex bit back a laugh, certain Dora would flinch if she saw her kitchen right now.

Water bubbled in a pan on the stove, a banana peel was draped partly off the counter. An orange juice carton vied for space on the table with several of Billy's toys, his bib and a half-finished bottle filled with the juice. Water waited in the glass container of the coffee brewer beside a can of coffee. On another counter, eggs were poised beside a bowl, plates and a loaf of bread. And then there she was, looking perfect with the sun spiking into the room and shimmering across the crown of her hair.

Audibly demanding attention, Billy released a sound that pierced the air like a banshee's cry.

"Just a minute," Carly promised. Looking back, she rolled her eyes at Alex. "You might not be hungry, but he is. Occupy him until I get his breakfast ready or he'll get cranky."

"Hey, Billy." Alex was rewarded with a greeting of a toothless grin. "You know, when I first met you, Carly, I didn't think you could cook," he said absently, bouncing Billy on his lap.

Not looking back, Carly poured oatmeal into the pan of water. "Why not?"

"There was nothing in your refrigerator at the apartment."

Over her shoulder, she sent him a look of disbelief. "You spied?"

Alex laughed as his son bounced up and down. "My son's welfare was at stake."

Exaggeratedly, Carly tsked. "I thought you were the honorable type."

"Yep." Amusement gleamed in his eyes. "And thorough, too."

"I had a good reason for the empty refrigerator. I was dieting then."

"Why?" he asked, looking at her with a lengthy sweep of admiration.

"Don't do that," she retorted lightly. "I can't concentrate when you look at me like that."

With Billy in his arms, Alex stood and peered over her shoulder at what she was stirring. "I'm not eating that."

Carly couldn't resist a tease. "I have mashed banana, too."

"I'll pass."

She dished out a bowl of oatmeal. "Now we know who Billy gets that obstinate streak from. Here." Carly thrust the bowl into his hand, then set the one containing bananas on the table. "You feed him. But alternate or he'll bubble the oatmeal back at you."

Alex grimaced at the mush in the bowls, then sat Billy in the high chair.

"Actually, he'll spit it at you." She laughed and whirled away to rummage through the cupboards. "It'll take me a few minutes to get our breakfast together. After all, this is Dora's domain."

"What are you cooking?"

"Trust me. You'll like it."

He'd been trusting her more than anyone else. She had no idea how much. "Okay, big guy, try one of these." On a chair near Billy, Alex stretched out his legs under the table and spooned oatmeal into his son's mouth. Never had he imagined himself doing this. Strangely, he'd done a lot of things he'd never done before because of one little boy—because of Carly. Even stranger, he'd enjoyed himself, whether playing cards with her, lazing in the sun and having breakfast or feeding his son.

Not cooperating, Billy puckered his lips and drooled out half the oatmeal.

Alex offered a spoon of bananas. "Now you get the good stuff."

"You're influencing him."

"I don't think so. He's pretty much his own man," he said as Billy nearly dumped the spoon of oatmeal in his efforts to push it away.

Carly cracked a smile and lifted the frying pan from the cabinet. Feeling like Indiana Jones with a great archaeological find, she raised the pan in the air as if waving a century-old treasure.

Alex didn't notice. "Vroom. Here it comes," he said in an airy tone meant to convince his son that the contents on the spoon was wonderful. Billy giggled his pleasure at the sound but gurgled out more oatmeal.

A sense of rightness swept over Carly that almost scared her. An ache filled her chest with longing. This is what she'd imagined when she'd thought of marriage, when she'd dreamed of family. But was it real? If she blinked, if she began to believe she'd found all that she wanted, would fate whisk it away from her?

"He ate it all," Alex said, snagging her attention. With satisfaction, he scraped the spoon across the bottom of the oatmeal bowl. "Does he do that for you?"

Carly dodged her own dark thoughts. Seeing Alex's smile of triumph, pleasure and amusement mingled within her. "Guess you're hired."

Alex carried the dishes to the sink. "I didn't do *that* well."

"Sure you did."

"No, I didn't," he said, suspecting that the flattery laid the way to a trap that would mean he got the questionable joy of feeding Billy the oatmeal every morning.

Carly flipped egg-coated bread in the pan, then shot a sideways glance at Billy. "He's hardly wearing any of it," she said, ignoring the smudges of oatmeal on Billy's cheek and the tip of his nose. "You did a wonder—" She squinched her head closer to her neck as Alex nuzzled her ear. "Wonderful job."

Soft. Her skin was soft as velvet everywhere. "Definitely." Unable to resist a fuller taste, Alex whirled her around to face him.

"Will you be home early?"

"Plan to," he assured her. Enjoying the warm sweetness of her, he mentally smiled. By then, he would have sprung his surprise on her.

Carly packed the dishwasher. With it and the washing machine running, she settled in her workshop for a couple of hours. In his playpen, Billy played with his latest fascination, a top-shaped toy with a musical carousel inside it.

Hours passed before she became aware of anything but the clay coming to life beneath her fingers. After days of unseasonable heat, a cool breeze brought relief and offered her a more bearable day in the small shed.

The chirping of a bird outside the shed roused her to glance at her wristwatch. After feeding Billy, she tucked him in for an afternoon nap. With the speaker for the baby monitor in one hand and a book in the other, she descended the steps, thinking about reading a few chapters of the medical thriller she'd started weeks ago.

She never sat down.

At the roar of engines, Carly flew to the window. Like a convoy, trucks rolled into the driveway and across the lush, green lawn toward the back of the property.

Carly dropped the book onto the table in the foyer and hurried outside. Like a child greedily delving into a mound of ice cream, the shovel of a bulldozer scooped a mound of dirt in the air, then dumped it into the back of one of the trucks. Carly dashed toward the closest truck to yell up at the driver. "What's going on?"

Unshaven and burly, his eyes snapped with impatience. The stub of a cigar clamped between his teeth, he mumbled a laconic response. "Digging a hole."

"I can see that." With relief, Carly noted that the digging wasn't disturbing the surrounding trees. "This is private property."

"Yes, ma'am." He chewed on the cigar stub. "But I've got an order here." He whipped a clipboard out the window to show her. "See?"

Carly stared at the address on the work order.

"Okay, lady?"

"Who signed it?"

"Got the feeling you would want more proof. Name's Herb," he said while rummaging through a stack of papers on the seat beside him. "Here's the original work order."

Carly stared at Alex's scrawled signature. "What are you digging the hole for? A pool?"

"Can't say." The driver guffawed. "Guess your old man's surprising you, huh?"

"Guess so," she answered. *But with what?*

* * *

Alex was late coming home. He'd reached the elevator more than an hour ago, only to be stopped by Doleman. With news for Carly, he wheeled his car into the driveway. The headlights shone on people strolling across it toward his backyard.

Moving swiftly, he bounded from the car and rushed across the grass toward the colored lights strung across the patio cover. He skimmed the sea of faces, all strangers.

"Hi, Alex." Hugging a huge bowl of what looked like potato salad, Adele beamed.

"Who are all these people?" he asked.

"Your neighbors. We're having a Block Watch party."

Alex opened his mouth, then shut it.

"Hi," a booming male voice said behind him.

Alex swung around. Immediately, the man pumped his hand. "I'm Bingerton. Beauregard Bingerton. Friends call me Beau. You do that," he said gregariously. "My wife, Peaches, and I live three doors away. Just moved here about a month ago—from Texas."

Alex would have guessed.

"You sure have one plum of a wife," Beau said. "We look at her as a daughter now."

A woman who barely reached his shoulder sidled close. Quickly, Beau introduced her. "Peaches, I was telling him how much we just love his Carly."

"We sure do," she said in an even thicker southwestern drawl. "And this is so nice, so neighborly, like back home."

Alex nodded. What else could he do? While the loquacious Beau went on about having sold all his cattle to his son before retiring to California, Alex swept his eyes over the grounds, searching for Carly. He couldn't see her anywhere.

A short while later, as he inched away from the Bingertons, he was cornered by a prune-faced, blue-haired woman he recognized. Alex had heard she'd left Nob Hill to escape the city, to find peace and quiet, and he prepared himself to endure her annoyance at all the commotion.

Instead, she gushed, "This is quite delightful. Crime is always on the rise, and now we have neighbors watching out for neighbors. It makes me recall the old days, the good ones, when you didn't have to lock your doors."

Again, Alex caught himself nodding.

Another couple tossed their names at him, and the man shook his hand. "We've never lived in a neighborhood before where people actually cared."

"Did you tell him what else we have planned?" his wife, a young yuppie asked. She didn't wait for his response. "We're discussing having a gigantic garage sale."

"A garage sale," Alex parroted.

The woman's smile widened. "Carly thought of it."

Of course, he mused, smiling. He excused himself as he located Carly standing near the buffet table.

"Love potlucks," some guy said in passing. Alex did a double take, certain he'd seen him delivering the mail. "Was that the postal carrier?" he asked as he reached Carly and motioned toward a thin man who was loading his plate.

"Say hello," she insisted, raising her face to him.

"Hello." A laugh colored his tone. "Was that our postal carrier?" he repeated.

Carly was grateful to see his smile. When he'd promised he would be home early, she'd thought she would have time to tell him about the party then. Having to spring it on him had sent a tiny flutter of anxiety through her. "That's who it is." She linked her arm with his and urged him around people sitting in chairs or on the lawn eating. "He's here with his wife and two kids. He's in the neighborhood all the time, so who else is better to keep an eye on our houses? It makes perfect sense."

"Perfect sense," Alex murmured and pulled her into the shadows of the trees. "I'm sorry I was late. I was on the way out the door when Doleman stopped me to invite us to dinner Monday evening. Think you can get a baby-sitter?"

Carly tugged at his tie. "Is there a reason for the invitation?"

"To announce the name of the new CEO." The smile in his eyes was filled with confidence. "Looks good."

Delighted for him, Carly flung an arm around his neck. "Alex, that's wonderful."

"Whoa." Laughter threaded his voice. "I haven't got it yet."

"You'll get it. You're the best one for the job."

Seeing her joy for him, he teased, "Then, am I forgiven?"

"For what?"

He rested his forehead against hers. "For being late. You thought the old Alex had crept back in when you weren't looking, didn't you?"

Carly saw no point in lying. "I had doubts."

"Don't have any." Because of her, he'd begun doing things for no other reason than enjoyment. "He's passé," he assured her lightly.

Amused by his words, she decided to test him. "Since you're in such a complacent mood, I'll warn you. That hole you ordered dug has totally demolished a portion of the backyard." Beneath the moonlight, her eyes gleamed with curiosity. "Herb wouldn't tell me what you're doing."

"Herb? Who's Herb?"

"One of the drivers. Probably the boss." Carly coiled both arms around his neck. "Want to tell me what they're doing?"

"It's a surprise."

"You're the one who's in for a surprise when you see the mess that used to be the lawn."

"I hate to interrupt." Adele's smile flashed in the darkness at them. "But it's time to start the meeting."

"Your adoring public awaits," Alex teased, slipping an arm around her waist.

Carly balked at being moved. "Alex, tell me."

Enjoying himself, he laughed. "Tell you later."

Carly's curiosity intensified. Every time she sneaked a look at Alex during the meeting, he merely grinned. He was putting her through agony, she mused as she said good-night to neighbors later. As a child, she used to shake Christmas presents, trying to guess their contents. She loved surprises, but lacked the patience to withstand the wait.

"It's later," she insisted when she strolled with Alex into their bedroom. "Tell me now what all those trucks were doing here." For added persuasion, she wiggled close to him.

With the subtle pressure of her body against him, Alex laughed at the swift need she aroused. "Are you trying to seduce an answer from me?"

She laughed softly and propelled him toward the bed. "Am I being successful?"

"Remarkably."

As he fell back, drawing her down with him, Carly set a hand to his chest to hold him off. He'd teased her inquisitive nature long enough. "What's going on? Why did they deliver lumber?"

"It's for your workshop. You'll have to pack up your stuff and—"

His words rang in her ears. Placing her hands on his face, she forced him to look at her. "My workshop," she repeated, feeling almost breathless. "Why? Why are you doing this?"

Though her eyebrows drew together, he saw the delight in her eyes, the stunned pleasure. Tenderly, he moved his lips down her throat. "You want reasons?"

Carly bit back a sigh. "Yes."

"You're talented. You'll be successful." Displaying persistence, he cupped a hand gently at her breast. "And I wanted to give you something that you wanted."

Her mind dueled with sensations from his hand's descent over her and the whisper of his lips across her shoulder blade. Raw emotion overwhelmed her. She wanted to believe in them. And love. Maybe she could believe she'd found that, too. "Why?" she asked on a long breath, her knuckles grazing his flesh as she tugged at his zipper.

Alex caught his breath. "Because you make me weak."

He couldn't say more. This time, no gentleness led them. She needed assurances; he needed to give them. They tugged clothes away, their movements hurried, almost desperate. Just as his mouth seduced, playing across hers until she forgot everything but him, his caresses taunted.

Lips clung together a moment longer. To her, all that mattered suddenly was his taste, the warm recesses of his mouth. Against her, she felt the hard beating of his heart, its rhythm quick and matching hers while his hands raced over her.

With a moan that echoed hers, they rolled on the bed. Kisses seared her skin. Something wild possessed her. She trembled with the pleasure. Passion was easy to deny. This need was different. Greedily, she touched him, reveling in the sleekness of his bare shoulders.

As his tongue circled her nipple, as his hands coursed over her in a fury of desire, she threw back her head, pressing it into the pillow beneath her and closed her eyes. Wherever he caressed, her skin warmed. Wherever his tongue stroked, her body tingled. When he scooted down, more warm kisses floating over her belly and thigh, she arched to meet his demand. She wished she could tell him all he meant to her, but she couldn't speak. Breathless, she moaned as she teetered at the edge of senselessness.

By the time his mouth took hers again, she'd stopped thinking. On fire, she fanned her hands over his buttocks. She wanted to tempt, to give, to pleasure. She wanted so much more than she dared hope for.

Muscles rippled in response to her slightest touch. With a graze of her fingertip, a slow, tantalizing stroke, she heard him gasp for air. Then she rolled with him again and sat up on her knees. Passion rushing around her, she caressed the body she'd become as intimately familiar with as her own, letting her fingertips flutter across his flesh to tease him.

Need mingling with want, she pressed her mouth to his chest, let her tongue moisten flesh while she traced the fine dark line of hair on his belly. She was his. Whatever he wanted, he could have.

Give. Receive. Pleasure. Her body hummed with it all. Moonlight pierced the room. Shadows danced across damp flesh. Craving blossomed.

She heard his breath shudder, then he rolled her to pin her beneath him. She needed to feel him filling her, to know the warm rush, the trembling pleasure that bound them. On a breathy whisper, she said his name. And as he took her again, her softness blended into him, and they strained against each other. Then waves of passion that promised madness swept over her.

Chapter Thirteen

"What time is the caterer coming?" Alex asked while he spooned coffee grounds into the brewer basket the next morning.

In comparison to the big party for his business associates, to Carly, the potluck party for neighbors had been a breeze. "This morning." She blocked her nervousness, not wanting him to see it, to share her doubts. "I invited a few friends. Adele and Willy and—"

"Willy?"

"The exterminator." As he swung a look at her, she laughed. "Alex, that's a joke."

He curled his upper lip and grunted a laugh.

Stirring scrambled eggs in a frying pan, Carly smiled to herself. The differences in their personalities always intrigued her. True, Alex's ambition bothered her sometimes, though she couldn't find offense with his success. His meticulousness annoyed her because it bordered on persnickety. In contrast, harmony always seemed boring to her.

And while she sensed he was a private man who relied on himself only, he'd made room in his life for her and Billy. Recently, the withdrawn man she'd married had given way to one who smiled quickly, whose laughter rippled on the air, whose passion left her breathless, who'd revealed a wonderful ability to laugh at himself. "I have a new outfit for tonight. Have you ever seen a belly dancer?"

Alex sidled close and nipped her earlobe. "You're full of mischief today, aren't you?"

"Get the laughs while you can."

"Are you implying that tonight's group is stodgy and humorless?"

"Aren't they?"

"Not nice."

Carly tsked and stared up at the ceiling as if something were written on it. "I could always think of something to liven up this party."

His chuckle rippled in her ear. He glanced at Billy, noticing his son's fascination with the cuff of his sleeper. "I don't suppose he'd let us go back to bed."

"Don't have time," Carly murmured on a laugh, but she wasn't unaffected by the tender play of his mouth. Seconds ago, the spatula had nearly slipped from her fingers when his lips had grazed the sensitive area below her earlobe.

"Sure we do."

"Really, we don't." She released a soft moan as his thumb brushed the edge of her breast. "Alex, really—"

"I'll clean Billy up," he promised as an incentive. "And do the dishes."

Carly sighed. "You offer an irresistible deal." Facing him, she parted her lips invitingly. "But we can't. Trucks," she managed to say between his quick, nibbling kisses. With the hand holding the spatula, she made a backhand gesture at the white van pulling into the driveway. "The caterer has just arrived."

Groaning, Alex slid his hands down her arms. "For the party."

"Tonight," she reminded him. Despite mustering up a smile and a light tone, every time she thought about the party that evening, an important one to him, her stomach knotted. If only Dora was around. She would know what was expected.

Alex had sensed nerves in her before he'd left for the office. He'd wished he could ease her mind. While he counted on everything going smoothly tonight—the caterer rarely botched the necessities—he doubted anything he said would have quieted Carly's anxiety.

"Alex?"

Looking up from the papers on his desk, Alex met the stare of J. T. Webb. Ruddy-faced and portly, the company's owner rarely showed up at the office. Golf and sailing interested him more since his retirement months ago. "See you this evening." Webb's gaze strayed to Alex's credenza. "That pottery is quite different, Alex. Where did you purchase it?"

"A gift from my wife." Amazingly, the word slipped over him with the same ease as a comfortable sweatshirt.

"Really?" Interest entered Webb's eyes. "My wife has a collection of pottery, Athenian, I think," he said with the air of an indulgent husband. "But she's always searching for new artists. Your wife is quite good."

Alex responded with a thank-you. He didn't need someone else to make him aware of Carly's talent.

The moment the caterers had arrived, Carly had taken command. She approached tonight's party with the same gusto she attacked any project. Though others might think she would leave everything to chance, her craft demanded a more disciplined and organized mind. She breezed between rooms to talk to the caterer and the bartender, to oversee the erecting of the white canopies in the garden, to direct the arrangement of flowers. After she gave her approval to the band's repertoire for the evening, she carried the folded playpen with one arm and ambled outside with Billy in her other arm.

Behind her, the wind flapped at the canvas of the tents. Ahead of her, a boy sat on the grassy knoll near the pond, slamming a baseball into his mitt.

The youngster's head jerked up, and a pretense at a smile spread his lips. "Are you the new neighbor?"

Carly snapped open the playpen and set Billy down with a musical ball. "No, I think you are," she said lightly, having earlier noticed the moving vans at the sprawling ranch several knolls away.

Looking sullen again, the boy shrugged a small shoulder. "Guess so."

The quick twist in Carly's heart urged her to linger.

His freckled nose wrinkled. "This is your property. Want me to go?"

"Nope." She plopped down beside him, bent her denim-clad legs and draped her arms around her knees. "Don't you like it here?"

"It's okay." Wind ruffled his light brown hair, sweeping it back from his face. "Mom says this is the last time we're moving. This time we're staying. I even joined Little League this morning."

Carly tipped her head to see his face. The glum expression remained. "So what's wrong?"

"I don't know anybody."

"You know me now. I'm Carly."

To Carly's relief, he gave her a quick smile as if he thought she was silly. "I'm Brian."

The soft spot in her heart for children had once made her consider teaching as a career. Of course, such a plebeian occupation for a Criswell was frowned upon. So Carly had done something even worse. She'd chosen the frivolous, financially unstable life of an artist. "Glad to meet you, Brian. I would like to meet your mom, but I can't come over today. We're having a big party, one of those business kinds."

"I know about them." He indicated they ranked at the bottom of his list of fun things to do. "We've had lots of them."

"This is my first." Carly met his stare. "I'm nervous."

His eyes widened. "Yeah?"

"Yes. But tomorrow, maybe I can meet your mom."

"You'll like her," he assured Carly. "She's nice."

"Your dad, too?"

The frown settled on his face again. "Him, too. But he isn't home. He's in Saudi Arabia, so me and Mom had to make the move alone."

Carly heard the loneliness for his father in the boy's voice. The image of her brother flashed in her mind. He'd been about Brian's age when their parents had died. He, too, had sat one day with a mitt in his hand. Miserable, he'd vented his anger by throwing the ball as hard as he could. Unfortunately, it had sailed through a neighbor's window. Only she had understood the confusion churning inside him about their parents' deaths, only she had been missing them as severely as he.

"You got any kids?"

Pressure in her chest swelled. "I have a son." She'd never said that to anyone before, she realized. *A son.* Billy wasn't just her nephew, he was her son now. No one could take that from her.

Interest rose in his voice. "Can he play ball?"

She snapped herself away from her thoughts. "He's too little." Swiveling a look over her shoulder, Carly pointed to Billy in the playpen. "He's a baby."

"Oh." For a second, he stared at Billy. With legs lifted, the baby was trying to tug off his shoe. "He's the only one?" Brian asked, not veiling disappointment.

"Yes, the only one." Carly eyed his brand-new mitt. "What position do you play?"

He beamed proudly. "Pitcher."

"Want to throw me a few?"

"You're a girl."

Carly laughed. "I can catch. Come on," she urged, gesturing with her thumb toward the grass behind them.

Hesitation was etched in his face. "I could use the practice. I got a game next week."

"So, what do you say?"

Again, he shrugged. "I guess."

Carly pushed to her feet. Only once did she glance toward the house and the people scurrying about. If she had stayed underfoot, she'd have caused a mutiny. One little boy was offering her a chance to relax. She needed that badly.

The sun had set before Alex was zipping his sports car onto the driveway. The sight of the caterer's van quieted some of his uneasiness. He hated being nervous. It made no sense to him; he'd entertained business associates before, and everything had turned out well.

Though he believed Carly would do her best, she was the difference this time. He wasn't certain what to expect from her. When he'd left this morning, as he'd always done with Dora, he'd relied on Carly to help organize the party.

Slamming the car door, he realized there was the crux of his jitteriness. Carly and organization didn't coincide. She liked to wing it. She seemed to thrive on spontaneity.

"Right in the center of the mitt," he heard her call out.

Curious and puzzled, Alex detoured toward the side of the house.

In a crouch, she held a baseball mitt in front of her, "Put it right in there, Brian."

Alex stared at her in disbelief. What was she doing? They had guests coming in less than an hour.

As the ball smacked into the mitt, Carly yelled out her encouragement, "That was a great fast ball."

It didn't take much for Alex to imagine her with Billy years from now. But with so much to do before the party, she'd clearly lost the order of things, or she wouldn't have been wasting time outside.

Whipping the ball back at Brian, Carly caught movement in her peripheral vision. "Got to go, Brian." She smiled for his sake, then met what she could only interpret as Alex's dark look. He was upset. She suspected she would cause that often just because she didn't do things the way he would. Doubts that she'd tried to ignore resurfaced. She might never fit into his life as perfectly as he might wish, as she might yearn to.

As she introduced Brian, Alex refrained from saying what was on his mind.

The boy shot him a crooked grin, then swung his round, freckled face up to Carly. "Will you play catch tomorrow, Carly?"

Faced with Brian's expectant gaze, Carly lightly touched his shoulder. "Tomorrow is fine."

"Great!" He sent her a sunny smile before he dashed off.

"He's a neighbor's boy." Carly disregarded the undercurrent of irritation hanging in the air between her and Alex. "His father is in Saudi Arabia right now on business and Brian's Little League game is next week," she said in a chatty manner. "He's pitching. Want to go and watch?"

Alex didn't like what he was feeling. She'd told him about a painful past, about people who'd treated her to some unhappy times because she'd failed them in some way. He felt like a carbon copy of them, but he had to consider the guests who would arrive in less than an hour.

"Think about going." Carly lifted Billy from the playpen. "It'll be fun."

Fun. Life involved more than fun. He'd counted on her to put this party together. Instead, she'd been in the yard playing catch with someone else's kid. Stupidly, he'd forgotten how easily she'd drifted from one project to the next while packing, how quickly she'd stopped to play with Billy or to follow her mood.

He'd forgotten something he'd vowed to remember years ago. Never rely on anyone. "What still needs to be done?" he asked, wondering if he could manage everything before the guests arrived.

"What makes you think anything does?"

Folding Billy's playpen, Alex considered how important the party was to his career. "If there wasn't, you would have been organizing everything. Instead, you're out here."

Carly's back stiffened at the hint of criticism tracing his voice. Something unexpected stabbed at her heart. The best course of action was to give Alex a wide berth. She didn't need him doubting her. She was worried enough about the party. Yet she couldn't ignore how easily his doubts about her had formed. "Alex." Carly counted slowly to ten. "Don't say any more."

Her warning jerked up his head. Hurt dulled her eyes. It didn't take genius IQ to know that unintentionally he'd helped some old feelings resurface within her. He muttered an oath. Hurting her was the last thing he'd meant to do. "What about an apology?"

Carly took in a shallow breath as their eyes locked. Hadn't she always believed that flaws as well as strengths made people interesting? Desperately, she wanted to back up the past few moments and play them over again. "Better than that. I'll pretend you didn't say anything," she said, because he was offering so much without confirmation that she hadn't disappointed him.

As she started to turn away, Alex caught her wrist. "Can you?"

Brushing her fingers across his jaw, she returned his smile. "Alex, just remember I'm not perfect."

So easily she gave so much. "Then we're a good match. Because obviously neither am I." Hooking an arm around her neck, he strolled with her down the hill to the back of the house.

The scene before him invited. White-jacketed servants hustled around, carrying out sparkling stemware. Flowers adorned an arched trellis. In the distance, he heard musicians tuning their instruments.

Why had he doubted her? More than once, she'd proven her stamina was endless. Hadn't he squared off against her never-quit attitude about Billy? A creative and talented potter, she'd somehow juggled a life that would exhaust most. Because she'd been with the boy, he'd made a dumb assumption that she'd neglected other responsibilities. "Looks like you haven't forgotten a thing." He tugged her tighter to him. "Thank you for doing this for me."

Crossing her fingers, Carly sent him a quick smile. "Don't thank me until it's over."

Half an hour later, Carly dangled an earring in her hand and meandered into the nursery. With the jacket of his tuxedo over the crib railing, Alex stood over Billy, grimacing.

"This is a doozy, son." On a quick intake of air, Alex used two fingers to pinch the soiled diaper, then holding it at arm's length, he dumped it.

Puzzlement etched his forehead as he slid a clean diaper under Billy's bottom. "Hell. How do you do this?" he muttered to himself, staring down at the diaper as if he were a neurosurgeon about to undertake a lifesaving operation.

Seconds later, as he drew back to view his accomplishment, Carly inched forward, catching his attention.

Alex lifted Billy from the soft pad of the changing table. "He needed his diaper changed, and—" Billy kicked his legs gleefully, sending the diaper sliding down to his ankles.

Carly pressed her head into Alex's chest, then gave up any solemn pretense and giggled.

"This is not funny."

"No, it isn't." She flicked the tie hanging at his collar. "You'd better finish dressing," she suggested on a laugh and stepped forward to refasten Billy's diaper. "I'll meet you downstairs."

"I'll look for the lady dressed for a harem," he teased and was rewarded by the sound of her laughter.

She took his breath away. She wore a simple black silk dress, something conservative yet elegant, something that would assure nods of approval, but she'd added a multicolored lamé jacket for flare. She would knock them out of their expensive shoes.

Alex joined her at the bottom of the stairs. As she drew a deep breath, the kind meant to calm anxiousness, he linked his fingers with hers and brought them to his lips to kiss her palm. "Just mingle." She smelled tempting, the fragrance lingering on her bringing to mind a sultry dark night and tropical flowers. "That's all you have to do."

"And wow them," she murmured airily, but a trace of nerves came through in her voice.

Alex followed her breezy stride as she swept into the living room. He didn't doubt for a moment that she would do just that. But they would only see her beauty; he'd been touched by it. From the first day he'd seen her holding his son protectively in her arms, he'd known how much she loved the child. The layers of her personality seemed immeasurable. She'd shown how lovingly maternal she was with Billy. She'd displayed concern and caring for a neighbor. She'd revealed youthful enthusiasm with a neighbor's youngster. And then there was the Carly he knew, the one who drove him mad with her seductive sexiness.

With one last survey of the living room, Carly placed a hand to her nervous stomach. She'd added only a touch of flowers. On a nearby buffet, the caterers had set out caviar, pâté and miniature quiches. Everything was ready, except her.

She jumped with a start at the sound of the doorbell and made herself join Alex near the door to greet their guests.

Minutes passed with introductions, small talk, pleasant chatter. The air filled with the scent of expensive perfume and the sound of ice cubes clinking in glasses. Men sporting tuxedos and women wearing the fashions of St. Laurent and Dior moved elegantly around the room and into the garden. Wealth surrounded Carly. She moved freely through the room, easing into conversations, charming, playing the perfect hostess with a panache that would have amazed her relatives.

Excusing herself from one group, she hurried upstairs to check on Billy in the nursery. When she returned to the party, she turned and found herself face-to-face with Diana Keenan. Sleek-looking, the brunette wore a classic white silk that bared one shoulder. "I understand that you have a hobby—pottery."

Carly racked her mind to remember the guest list. Nowhere had she seen the woman's name listed. "Actually I plan to open my own business."

Diana tipped her head up to deliver a down-the-nose look at Carly. "How convenient for you then."

"I beg your pardon."

"How convenient then that you married Alex. With his social contacts, my dear, your career will blossom."

"I see you've met my niece," a feminine voice said to Carly's right.

Carly forced a semblance of a smile for Leone Pipperton. Obviously, the older woman was responsible for Diana's appearance, thinking nothing about letting her niece tag along. "Yes, I have."

Leone's lips spread in a polite plastic smile. "Would you excuse us? Diana, I want you to meet Hubert's son."

"She's rather ordinary," Diana said haughtily in a not-too-soft voice as she stepped away with her aunt.

"Regardless, Diana, she did a magnificent job tonight. Did you taste the walnut biscotti?"

"Thank the caterer," Diana quipped snidely.

"I was told that it was her recipe. She insisted on it being served along with the shrimp—"

"Auntie Leone, she hardly came from a farm. She's Victoria Van Mern's black-sheep niece. She would be the kind to trap Alex into marriage."

Was that what everyone thought? Carly wondered, watching them thread their way to the buffet table and the councilman's son.

Needing a moment alone, she sidestepped couples to wander onto the terrace. A step from the door, a man barred her path. The turmoil inside her intensified as she stared at a face from her past. "Christian, what a surprise."

Still lanky, Christian Van Mern's face looked almost gaunt. "Carly." As if the gesture was obligatory, her cousin brushed her cheek with his. "You haven't called mother," he said, giving her a look filled with the arrogance of power.

"Is Aunt Victoria well?" On edge, Carly snatched a champagne flute from the tray of a white-jacketed servant passing by, then reconsidered drinking it and handed it to Christian.

"I'll tell her that I saw you," he said instead of answering her.

Carly managed a slip of a smile. To her relief, the reunion was short-lived. Spotting the councilman, he wandered off to sandwich himself between him and Doleman. Carly wished the party was over. She longed for silence. She wanted to be upstairs holding Billy.

From across the room, Alex inched his way to her, wondering about her sudden paleness. As he reassuringly placed a hand at the small of her back, her tension penetrated his palm. The reason for it came quickly as Carly explained that Christian was her cousin. "I was told that he and Diana crashed the party together."

Carly struggled to lighten her own mood. "And here I thought he was Mr. Manners."

Though aware they'd garnered the attention of a few guests, Alex was less concerned with the others. What bothered him more was the strain in her voice. "Have you called your aunt?"

"No, I haven't." She looked away, thinking about the phone call she'd nearly made. "I told you. She wouldn't want to talk to me."

Alex wished he could erase the troubled frown in her eyes. He wanted to offer anything he could, anything that would help as he deduced that she'd only breezed over her past before this. Behind smiles, she hid a torment that had lingered, the pain of a child who'd felt unloved.

"Adele's having a good time," Carly said, signaling the subject was closed.

Alex looked at Adele fluttering around, then zeroed in on a strange-looking guy with three earrings and a lion's mane of dark hair who was waving his hands around Leone's head. "Carly, who's that?"

"That's Raphael, a neighbor from the next block. He opened a new hair salon. I met Julia outside his shop when I was in San Francisco." She beamed up at him. "I thought he might get some business if he came to the party. Is that a problem?"

"No problem." How could he have any? If she was pleased, nothing else mattered. He had more happiness in his life now than he'd ever imagined—because of her.

"It went well," Carly said when the last of their guests finally went out the door.

Alex closed and locked it, then slid an arm around her waist. "Very well."

In stocking feet, Carly dangled her shoes and started climbing the stairs. She wanted to go with the moment, forget some of the less comfortable encounters of the evening, but she couldn't forget one. "Isabel Webb has commissioned me to make something for her. Did you—" Carly struggled with the right words as she preceded him into the bedroom. She tossed her head as if trying to shake free the tension of the past few hours. "I know our original arrangement included your helping me with my career, but I don't—"

"No one needs to help you." Barely touching her shoulder, Alex stilled her to unzip her dress. "Your talent speaks for itself."

Carly stared in the mirror and pridefully raised her head. "Whispers said differently."

Alex wanted to laugh that she'd paid any attention to party gossip, but the seriousness in her eyes had to be considered. "Someone said something?"

"Yes. Leone Pipperton's niece. Diana."

"I would have expected that." Head bent, he drew down the zipper then turned her to face him. "They formed a conspiracy from the first day I met Diana. Leone expected me to marry her niece," he said honestly. He didn't want her to learn that bit of information through idle chatter.

The reminder stirred a pang of sadness in Carly. Would Alex have married Diana if she hadn't made him choose between her and Billy? Disturbingly, Carly had to consider that she was a substitute for the woman he might have fallen in love with.

Alex saw what appeared to be pain on her face. "That never would have happened," he assured her. "One look at you and the rest paled." He'd spoken the truth, suddenly alert to how thoroughly enchanted he was with his wife.

Carly wanted to cling to his words, to his smile. Did she dare? "So you say," she teased, to stop herself from getting more serious than him.

"Don't believe me?" Alex kissed the base of her throat. "Doesn't matter." Before she could grab a breath, he cupped a palm at the back of her head so her face was closer. "I'll prove it," he murmured against her mouth and drew her down to the bed with him.

Only one word described what Alex felt. *Whole.* Languidly, he twined a strand of her hair around his finger while he drew steadying breaths and listened to the pelting of the rain against the window.

Lightly, Carly nibbled at his shoulder. "I'm hungry. Want something?" She eased from him to crawl out of bed, then slipped into her kimono-style wrap.

Alex murmured unintelligibly.

"Is that yes or no?" she asked, bending over him.

Intimately, he slid a hand over her bottom. "Stay."

"If I promise to come back, will you—" She paused and laughed as his tongue dipped in her ear. "I'll come back."

In a reluctantly slow move, Alex withdrew his hand from under her robe. "Hurry."

Her sound of pleasure rippled to him. His eyes half-closed, he stretched and turned his face into the pillow. Her scent lingered, seeping into him. He'd never believed in the closeness he'd begun to find with her. Because of his parents, he'd seen the destructive force of love. He'd always believed it was better to stand alone. Yet, she'd become important to him. In a short time, she'd filled an emptiness he'd been unaware of. She made each day special. She'd made him do something he'd never foreseen—she'd made him fall in love. Love. The idea amazed him.

Nudging himself from the bed, he grabbed his jeans from a nearby chair, then padded downstairs. "What did you find?" he asked upon entering the kitchen.

Everything, Carly thought. Through the wet glass of the kitchen window, she peered at the tarp draped over the lumber for her new workshop. Turning, she shot a smile at him. "I haven't looked for anything yet."

"Here I expected a feast waiting for me."

"Foolish man."

At the rumble of thunder, Alex leaned closer to the window and waited for the streak of lightning. Rain held special memories, he realized. "Take off your slippers."

Palming a head of lettuce, Carly swung a puzzled look at him. "Take off my—" A giggle slipped out as he knelt before her. "What are you doing?" she asked on a laugh when he curled fingers around her ankle and lifted her leg to slide off her slipper. "Are you going to tell me why you're doing that?"

"Live a little," he teased laughingly while removing her other slipper.

"This is odd behavior." Carly cracked a smile. "Are you drunk, Alex?" she asked at the crown of his dark head.

Intoxicated by her, he thought whimsically and grabbed her hand to draw her with him out the door.

"Come on," he urged, dashing out from under the terrace cover.

The rain sprayed at her face, tingled her skin. Carly tossed back her head and laughed. "I thought you didn't like to walk in the rain."

As the wind blew at her hair, he caught it and held it back. "With you I do," he said softly. On the damp air, her fragrance drifted to him. Rain pelted them now, plastering her hair to her head, darkening it.

God, but it would be so easy to believe in them. He couldn't pretend any longer that only their feelings for Billy connected them. He'd wanted her. But that only skimmed the surface of the emotion she churned inside him. A tightness swelled in his chest. She, only she, did what no other person had; she made him care.

"You look like a drowned puppy," she said with a laugh.

"Flattery will get you everywhere." Tenderness filling him, he pulled her closer. "I love you, Carly."

She stopped breathing, certain she'd misunderstood him. "What did you say?" she asked, blinking rain out of her eyes.

In them, Alex saw the struggle within her. "I said I love you."

How simple he made it sound. Yet those words from him meant so much. She knew that he'd believed loving someone meant promises that usually were broken. And he was offering it, trusting her to be there when need arose. None of that had anything to do with passion. It had to do with the heart, with the soul, with feelings. And he was giving it all to her.

The steady rhythm of the rain offered a musical beat that matched the accelerated one of her heart. In his quiet way, he'd already accepted so much about her, despite quirks that other people had always exasperatedly shaken their heads at.

A flash of lightning illuminated his face, sweeping across his cheekbones, a portion of his jaw. This was their beginning, she realized. She would have more than a marriage of convenience. She would have love. She would have it all—with him. Love with no conditions. "I love you," she said softly because her heart was open to him.

The wind whirled, rustling trees. Alex wasn't aware of it. As her breath mingled with his, he had one more thought before the mist of sensation floated over him. No one had ever said that to him before.

Chapter Fourteen

Outside the kitchen window, morning clouds crowded the sky with the threat of more rain. Sipping his coffee, Alex shifted on the chair and curiously fingered a three-ring binder Carly had left on the table. In amazement, he explored what he assumed was Carly's work journal. Inside, she'd jotted notes, pages of them, about the time of firing, the temperature, the cooling time for her pottery. On other pages, she'd categorized pots completed, designs, drawings, results of glaze tests. Everything was organized.

She was a bit of a fake. Despite some quirky behavior and what seemed like a tendency to flit from one project to the next, she approached her work like an efficiency expert.

Vying for Alex's attention, Billy banged a plastic set

of keys against the high-chair tray and blew out spit bubbles.

At the sight of drool staining the front of the baby's T-shirt, Alex hunted in the stack of unfolded laundry on the kitchen table for one of Billy's clean shirts. He chose the first one he found and eased Billy's rubbery arms into a shirt sleeve. The shirt had Tweety on the front of it.

"Consider it a furthering of your education," Carly had teased days ago. Then she'd proceeded to identify for him several other cartoon characters like Garfield and Big Bird and Sylvester.

Just the kind of information to keep an executive ahead of everyone else, Alex reflected, before pivoting to reach for the ringing phone.

Holding his palm against his son's chest to keep him in place, he had to stretch for the receiver. "Hold it a minute," he said instead of a greeting.

Whoever was on the other end better have patience and a sense of humor. Seconds ticked by while Billy squirmed and warbled a protest.

"You have to put your other arm in." Alex shook his head. Reasoning didn't work with a seven-month-old. That was something else he'd learned. As quickly as he could, Alex snapped the front of the shirt and fastened Billy back in the chair.

"Ssh," he soothed, kissed his son's cheek and tucked the plastic keys in the boy's chubby hand, even demonstrating how to bang them. Billy needed no further instructions. Merrily, he resumed clanging them against the plastic in a steady rhythm.

Grasping the receiver, Alex hoped he wouldn't hear Webb or Doleman and especially not Leone Pipperton's voice responding. "Sorry."

"Hi, yourself," Dora said on a laugh. "What's going on?"

"Billy spit up. I was changing his shirt." He laughed. "I won."

Dora chuckled. "Quite an opponent, huh?"

"The toughest I've ever met." Alex cast a glance out the window.

Laughing and talking, Carly stood with their new neighbor near the pond. Like her son Brian, Lisa Robets revealed a hunger for new friends. Earlier, she'd shown up looking for her son, who was throwing curve balls to Carly. A petite brunette with a heart-shaped face, a sprinkling of freckles and cheerleader looks, she'd invited them over for dinner next week. The refusal Alex had nearly uttered had remained silent as Carly had enthusiastically accepted, even offering to help Lisa unpack.

Alex zeroed in again on Dora's groaning about the rain in Bangor while he narrowed his eyes to see what Lisa was handing Carly. Too far away, he gave up immediately. "Not having fun?" He cradled the receiver between his jaw and shoulder and began folding Billy's pajamas.

"I'm making tea for the queen," Dora said, referring to her sister.

"I'm folding laundry," Alex told her on a laugh.

Dora cackled in his ear. "That's an image I'll carry with me all day." She laughed again, sounding totally relaxed.

Alex ceased his search for a matching sock in the laundry basket. "How's your sister?"

"Cranky. That means she's better."

The quiet behind Alex made him swivel a look at Billy. His son was gnawing on his fist with a fascinated expression on his face. "When are you coming home?" he asked while uncapping a jar of pears.

"Soon. I can hardly wait to see the new you."

He couldn't deny he'd changed. Not once during his climb up the ladder of success had he visualized himself folding baby clothes or considering the ingredients in pureed food or changing a stinky diaper.

By the time Carly opened the door, Alex had begun spooning the pears into Billy's mouth.

"Look what I have," Carly said brightly and swept a pan covered with aluminum foil beneath his nose.

Alex followed the smell. "What's that?"

She lifted the foil to reveal brownies. "They're from Adele. She brought some over for Lisa and Brian, and gave her a pan for us." Carly put the pan on the kitchen counter, then after taking Billy's bottle from water warming there, she shook white drops on the underside of her wrist.

"I'll give the bottle to him," Alex offered, taking it from her. "Her trouble hasn't stopped, has it?" he asked while lifting Billy into his arms.

Carly's smile dimmed. "I don't think it will, either. Vestor wants her property badly, although I don't think he's the buyer. I think he's someone else's muscle man. The problem is, the police aren't big about handling harassment. But something has to be done to stop him."

Alex shifted his sleepy son to his shoulder. "By you?" he asked quietly, standing. She faced him with a stubborn look that was becoming familiar.

"Alex, I'll do whatever I can. I promised her that I would be with her if she needs me." Carly had assumed that, given his past, he would understand the importance of keeping her word to Adele.

He said no more on the subject and offered the bottle to Billy. "Don't forget to meet me after you leave the pediatrician's today."

Circling the kitchen, Carly checked the soil of her plants, then sprinkled water on a philodendron. "You still won't tell me why."

"Can't," he said, sliding his fingers down the bottle so Billy could wrap his chubby hand around it.

"Won't," she countered.

"Both." Glancing up, he delivered his best persuasive smile. "Just meet me," he insisted and rattled off the address.

"Mysterious, aren't you?"

"I'm trying to tarnish my predictable, inflexible image. How am I doing?"

"You're making headway," she assured him as he set Billy in his high chair.

"Is that the best you can do?"

A laugh slipped out at his feigned crestfallen look. "Okay, you're becoming Mr. Spontaneity." The idea seemed so ludicrous, she couldn't help laughing. Every night, he chose the clothes for the next day and hung them on the valet, and he always picked up the mail the moment he entered the house. He even made a peanut butter and jelly sandwich in exactly the same way every time.

"I heard doubt in your voice. Who took you for a walk in the rain? And who brought cheese and crackers to bed the other night?" he reminded her.

Carly gasped as he snaked his arm around her waist and whipped her around to face him. "You did."

"Damn straight."

His cheek to hers, he led her in a quick interpretation of a tango, twirled her out and back and ended with an exaggerated dip that bent her backward. "And has anyone else ever done this with you?"

Choking back a giggle, Carly collapsed against his arm. "Only you," she managed to say between bouts of full-blown laughter.

After Alex left, Carly considered the day ahead of her. A phone conversation earlier that morning with J. T. Webb's wife had skyrocketed excitement through her. Isabel Webb wanted more than Carly had first thought. A collector of Greek pottery, the woman had requested a replica of a Mycenaean drinking cup. The challenge thrilled Carly. But then, challenge always did.

Thinking about her drive to the city, she shivered during her stroll to her car. A wind that whipped branches and rolled heavy pewter-colored clouds across the sky rushed around her. Carly mentally groaned at the thought of more rain. With luck, she would be back from the pediatrician's appointment and the mysterious meeting with Alex before the weather changed.

Another stubby cigar in his mouth, Herb stuck his head out the truck window. "See you tomorrow, Carly."

Carly looked away from setting Billy in his car seat and waved as she slipped behind the steering wheel. She hoped that later in the afternoon she would have time to visit some ceramics galleries that might take pottery on consignment by an unknown. Earlier, she'd lost some time searching for the newspaper. She'd never found the real estate section that listed buildings for rent. She was anxious to open a shop from which she could sell her pieces. Yesterday, she'd pondered over the columns of print and had neatly circled those that had interested her. If she picked up another newspaper, she might have time to scan it while she was waiting in the doctor's office.

Behind his desk, Alex swore as he knocked over a stack of reports while reaching for the ringing phone. A glance at the clock assured him Ginnie was on her lunch break. Distracted, stretching to the side for the strewn papers, he offered a greeting.

"Mr. Kane, this is Victoria Criswell Van Mern," the woman announced as if she were the queen of England.

Alex straightened slowly.

"Carly's aunt," she added.

"Yes, I know."

"I learned from my son that Carly is living in California again."

Alex leaned back in his chair and reined in a temper that was precariously close to slipping away from him. With her unfeeling manner, this woman had inflicted too much hurt on Carly. He took a leveling breath, deciding to reserve judgment until he learned why she'd called. Schooled to know when to talk and when to keep quiet, Alex remained silent. It's your quarter, lady, he mused.

"I'm calling because I would like to talk to my niece. Do you think she would want to talk to me?"

Plenty of times, he wanted to say, but refrained from speaking his mind. "I assume she would. But she isn't home. She's at the pediatrician's office."

"And who would that be?" Self-importance oozed from her.

Alex hesitated. How would Carly react to a surprise visit from an aunt who'd given her a minimum of attention? He weighed his decision for only a second, then gave her the doctor's name.

At her brisk goodbye, Alex stared at the receiver in his hand, then quickly punched out the number for the pediatrician's office. "I'm trying to reach my wife," he said to the bubbly-sounding receptionist.

"Mrs. Kane is in the office with the doctor. Is it an emergency?"

What if her aunt didn't show? Then she'd be disappointed. "No, it isn't. Never mind," he said and dropped the receiver back in the cradle. With a glance, he checked his calendar for the day. He had one meeting he had to attend. The rest of his appointments could wait. If Carly needed him, he wanted to be there for her.

In the reception room of the pediatrician's office, Carly sidestepped a two-year-old who was bent over, attempting a headstand. Billy peered over Carly's arm at the little girl. "You'll get to do that soon enough," Carly said lightly, pleased he'd braved the immunization shot so well.

Lunch on her mind, she stepped outside and eyed a restaurant across the street well-known for delicious, greasy hamburgers.

"You look quite well, Carly," a feminine voice said behind her.

Carly spun around.

Wearing a steel blue suit, silk blouse and a string of pearls, her aunt looked as refined as always. More gray threaded her dark hair now, but she still carried herself like a woman a decade younger than her sixty-nine.

"Aunt Victoria." Stunned, nothing else would come out.

As a greeting, her aunt brushed Carly's cheek with her own. "You truly do look quite lovely."

And probably surprised. Carly wondered if she was gaping.

"Christian told me he saw you the other night at the home of Alexander Kane."

Vowing not to be intimidated, she corrected, "My home."

"Yes, he told me that also." Her pale blue eyes shifted to Billy. "This is the boy?"

Instinctively, Carly tightened her hold on him. "Yes, Randy and Emily adopted him."

"So you said at their funeral." Her cursory glance at Billy pricked Carly. "Perhaps you have time for tea."

Though she couldn't imagine what would be gained, Carly's curiosity was too piqued to refuse. "Yes, I do."

"Very good. We'll have tea at the nearby hotel. I have my car."

Memories of sitting prim and proper because of a caveat from her aunt not to wrinkle her clothes flashed back at Carly. She'd never liked those gray limousines. "Mine is parked outside. I'll meet you there."

Her aunt's back straightened. "Always a mind of your own."

For an instant, Carly nearly slipped backward and made an excuse to soothe her aunt's displeasure. "I need to go to my car, anyway," she said. What she badly needed was a place to change Billy's diaper.

"Very well. I'll meet you."

The hotel's tea room was elegant, unbearably quiet and terribly staid. Ladies lunched on finger sandwiches and carried on conversations in hushed tones. Only the soft buzz of their voices and the occasional clinking of silverware broke the stifling silence. The atmosphere definitely wasn't conducive to the wail of a baby.

As Carly set Billy beside her in his carrier seat, he squirmed slightly, then yawned. If she was in any luck, he would snooze through this spontaneous tea party.

"We never received an invitation to your wedding," her aunt said crisply.

Carly couldn't imagine her aunt standing in the Las Vegas chapel with its artificial pink flowers and out-of-tune piano. "We married on the spur of the moment."

"So like you."

Carly stifled a frown. Inadequacies born in her childhood shadowed her. For so long, she'd wanted this woman to accept her, to embrace the person she was. It'll never happen, she thought in resignation. She would never measure up to her aunt's expectations.

"However, I'm pleasantly surprised by your choice."

Carly felt a ridiculous mixture of both pleasure at her aunt's approval and annoyance that she still cared what the woman thought.

"I saw Bennett Doleman yesterday. He's quite impressed with your husband. Wherever did you meet him?"

"I thought you knew. He's Billy's biological father."

"Is he?" She was silent a second. Carly could imagine the thoughts racing through her aunt's mind. "And you quickly fell in love with him?"

The hint of criticism in her tone came through clearly. Perhaps it wouldn't start their lunch off well, but Carly saw no point in pretending. "We married for several reasons."

Confusion sharpened her aunt's pale eyes. "Reasons?"

"Yes, there were reasons," Carly said flatly.

"My, that's a surprise." Slowly, she stirred her tea. "I assumed, well, in the past, you were always ruled by your emotions."

Too many years of being criticized in exactly the same way rallied youthful defiance. "I still am." She looked up from the tea in her cup and told her aunt only the facts. "We entered into this marriage because of Billy." If they were closer, Carly might have shared more and explained how frightened she'd been of losing Billy, how much love she'd found so unexpectedly. "And Alex needed a wife because of his career."

Puzzlement marred her forehead. "Well, regardless of the reasoning behind this union, I am pleased you've done so well."

Carly released an impatient sigh. Why did a compliment from her sound so belittling? Happy with her life, she'd forgotten the pressures and demands she'd left behind.

Her aunt's thin lips spread in a semblance of a smile. "How many times did I tell you no, and you'd do what you wanted, not worrying about the consequences of your impetuous actions? You had such a mind of your own."

Carly lifted an eyebrow. If she hadn't known better, she might have imagined admiration for her in her aunt's tone.

"You were always so full of life. My sister was like that."

Disbelief swept over Carly at the soft, almost affectionate sound she'd heard.

"Sometimes, it was quite painful to look at you." As if annoyed at the hint of real emotion overcoming her, Victoria blinked quickly to mask another second of true feeling. "When she was gone, I missed her terribly. I hope you understand."

The child Carly had left behind might never understand. She, too, had lost. Her parents, the people who'd meant the most to her, had disappeared from her life. She'd needed to know someone loved her. She and Randy had desperately wanted to feel someone's arms around them. But they'd only had each other.

"We tried to give you everything," Victoria said. She delivered a tight smile. "Now that is all part of the past, though, isn't it?"

Carly lifted her chin a notch and battled the fresh hurt. The woman she was comprehended. When she'd lost Randy, someone dear to her, she'd nearly folded inside herself. The pain had seemed unbearable at times. But she'd hung on. For the child he'd loved, she'd gone on. She'd fought to give Billy everything Randy would have. No, she didn't think she'd ever truly understand her aunt turning away from the two children who'd needed her and not giving them what they'd needed most—love.

"Now, however, I assume you're wondering what I want. It's quite simple. I would like to see you more often."

Carly's heart opened. "You would like to visit Billy and me once in a while?"

"You," she said crisply. "I would like to visit you. He's not really one of ours, is he?"

All the hope faded in an instant. Sadness rushed in, deep within, for this woman who didn't fathom the true meaning of love. "Yes, he is."

Her aunt's forehead wrinkled in a frown.

"Randy loved him," Carly felt compelled to remind her. "Love is what makes a child a part of you," she said, wondering if she was wasting her time saying words that seemed so obvious to her, but that must carry a concept so foreign to her aunt. "And he's very much one of ours."

"I see."

By her tight-lipped expression, Carly expected her aunt to rush to her feet, but she remained sitting.

"You said he's Alexander Kane's son?" she asked as if that might make Billy more acceptable. Of course, Alex would meet her aunt's standards perfectly—rich, successful and influential.

"Yes, he is."

"He has made quite a name for himself. I suppose that I should spend more time with the boy, then," she said placatingly.

A refusal hung on the tip of Carly's tongue.

"Actually, I would like to know your family," Victoria said.

More aware than anyone of the effort her aunt was making, Carly took the extra step to meet her halfway. She reached forward for her aunt's hand.

For an instant, she stiffened. Carly ached for the years lost, for the closeness she would never have with this woman who was so like her mother yet so different.

"Then we'll meet again." Her manner was stiff and formal as if she were talking to an acquaintance instead of family.

Carly sighed in resignation but nodded agreeably. Alone, she took time to finish her tea. They'd bridged the anger, but so much would always keep them at a distance.

When she stepped outside minutes later, she kissed Billy soundly for being a perfect angel, then fastened him in his car seat.

Rounding the front of her car, she spotted a balloon vendor. She definitely needed something to lift her spirits.

Alex was waiting for her at the agreed-upon corner. His back against the wall of a building, he watched her sprightly step as she pushed Billy's stroller and the three balloons tied to it bobbed in the air. "Where did you get the balloons?" he asked, pushing away from the building to meet her.

"They're a treat. One's for Billy, one's for me and there's one for you."

"For me?"

Carly mustered up a bright smile. "That's right."

He slid an arm around her waist and kissed her cheek. "What are we celebrating?"

"An awakening. When I was young, I always thought everything was my fault. It wasn't." Carly leaned into him and explained. "My aunt showed up out of nowhere."

Her smile didn't fool him. It was strained by the shadow of concern dulling her eyes. Ever since her aunt's call, he'd been waiting and wondering how the meeting had gone. "She called me, Carly. I didn't know if you would want to talk to her."

"When I first saw her, neither did I," Carly said, bending to retrieve the stuffed giraffe Billy had tossed out of his stroller.

"How did it go?"

Carly recalled the vague criticism in her aunt's voice before her departure.

"Don't lose my number," she'd said sharply as if Carly were a dolt.

Carly doubted her aunt would ever really change. "For us, it went well."

At her weary sigh, Alex wished now he'd been there for her. "That's good news," he said cautiously and slipped a hand under her elbow to urge her to walk with him.

"It's an improvement." With effort, she thought she and her aunt might manage a semblance of closeness. As Alex's grip tightened, she turned questioning eyes up at him. "Where are we going?"

"Here." His hand at her shoulder, he aimed her in the direction of an empty building. "What do you think?"

Confusion made her laugh. "Think about what?"

Alex reached around her and opened the door. "Where's your imagination?" he teased.

Carly shuffled forward beneath the light pressure of his hand at the small of her back. "About what?"

"Is the location good? Does the light shine through the window right? Is it big enough? What name are you going to put on the sign?"

"Mine?" Carly turned in his arms. "How did you know I was looking?"

Grinning, Alex whipped a folded newspaper from his back pocket.

"I looked all over for this," she said, flicking a finger at the paper in his hand.

"You would have never found it." Amusement danced in his eyes. "I hid it."

"You—"

With a quick kiss, he silenced her words. "So what do you think?" he asked, swinging her around again to examine the space. "Do you like it?"

She could easily envision several vessels in the window, the morning sunlight catching their highly glossed glazed finishes. "Yes," she said, feeling stunned. The location was perfect, the small store nestled between galleries at the top of a hill. It was everything she'd always longed for.

At her silence, Alex tipped his head to see her face. Emotion swirled inside him. At what point had her energy, her joy, her spirit had such a contagious effect on him? Like a magnet, she drew him to her, tugged him along until he was doing more than he'd ever expected. And he felt contented because she soothed the tension in him. She made him laugh. She made him want to believe in something he'd shied away from all his life.

She'd made him love. "You'll probably need help here." At her unusual speechlessness, he laughed with pride of accomplishment at surprising her.

Scanning the brightly lit room with its wall of windows, Carly's heart swelled with joy. "You're always one step ahead of me."

"Is that bad?"

Carly gave him a beaming smile. "No, it's wonderful. You've been wonderful," she added, sliding her hands up his back. "But I never expected all of this."

Alex tightened his embrace. No, she never expected anything. Giving is what she did with the natural ease with which others drew a breath. "You might want to find someone to manage it." Her heart filled with a happiness that almost scared her. She'd never had what she wanted in life, and now, suddenly, she had everything. "Alex, you give me too much."

"Never enough. Never," he whispered and lowered his head to kiss her.

Before heading home, Carly stopped and bought a new dress for the evening's festivities at Bennett Doleman's home. She couldn't remember a more perfect day. True, the time with her aunt hadn't been comfortable. But at least they'd eased some of the tension that had existed between them for decades. Carly still had misgivings about their relationship improving. Her aunt had fashioned herself to be cool and withdrawn, believing too many smiles, too much genuine warmth would weaken her.

With the portable phone beside her in her workshop, she considered the work ahead of her on Mrs. Webb's drinking cup. For authenticity, Carly planned to use the ancient technique for firing the piece. First, she would fire it in an open kiln so it would turn red. Then, in a closed kiln, the cup would turn black. When she did the final stage, the kiln would be opened a little to let in enough oxygen to turn the thinner coating of the slip red again. Thus, she would achieve the red and black decoration so often used during that time in history.

Stretching, she considered the contractor's progress on her new workshop. She almost felt the need to pinch herself, but she wasn't dreaming. She would soon have a workshop and a store in which to sell her work. All she needed was a manager.

Grabbing the telephone, she punched out a long-distance number. She listened to several rings before a familiar voice responded with an enthusiastic hello.

"Renee, would you still want to manage my shop?"

"You're opening it!" she said with an excitement Carly had hoped to hear.

"Yes, it's no longer a pipe dream. Are you still interested?"

"I would love to come. I need to get my kid sister away from Biff, the king of the bikers."

Carly laughed. "Oh, I've missed you."

"Ditto. So how was this possible so soon?"

"Alex," she answered because that said it all.

A short while later, strolling back to the house, Carly lifted her face toward the setting sun. A cement mixer whirled, drowning out the usual chirping of birds. At dawn, the workers had arrived to lay the foundation for her studio.

She'd already envisioned a bench near the wheel for freshly thrown pots, a table for glazing, shelves to hold ware ready for firing, a place for a wedging board and another table for the scales. With the image of her studio so vivid in her mind, she felt some disappointment that she had too much to do to spend time working.

"See you tomorrow," Herb yelled from his truck window. "Did you find out what the surprise was?"

"I did." She flashed him a smile. "And it's wonderful."

His cheeks bunched like a chipmunk's. "Glad to hear it."

"See you."

With Billy fed and changed, Carly showered then dressed. Midnight blue, the scoop-necked dress she'd chosen shimmered and sparkled with her every movement. While purchasing it, she'd considered how important this evening might be to Alex. Perhaps it was seeing her aunt again that made her jittery, made her remember all the times she'd committed some faux pas during her youth, made her jump as the phone rang.

Alex was the last person she'd expected a call from. "Hi, yourself. I'm in a bind," he said, but she heard the smile in his voice. "I have a late meeting. Could you meet me at the party?"

"Sure." Her breezy response veiled her anxiety. The idea of entering Doleman's home alone escalated her jitters about tonight. On an uncharacteristic oath, she straightened her shoulders. She wouldn't do anything wrong. And she wasn't nervous, she told herself firmly.

At another trill of the phone, she spun around. Liar, her mind screamed. Snatching up the receiver, she laughed, and said, "Hello."

"Carly."

Adele's strained tone instinctively tensed Carly. She supposed anyone dependent on a baby-sitter would feel the same apprehensive flutter. But if Adele reneged on her promise to baby-sit, Carly faced a real problem. She couldn't call Lisa Robets; she and Brian had merrily driven off to the airport to pick up Lisa's husband, Gordon. "What's wrong?"

"Carly, he said he's coming here."

"Who?"

"That despicable man. Vestor," she practically cried. "What should I do?"

Carly contemplated the problem. So Vestor had altered his scare tactics, probably because Adele hadn't become unnerved by his harassing phone calls. A confrontation provided more possibilities for his terrorizing her. "You need to call the police," Carly said, relying on Alex's reasoning. He believed the sight of them might deter Vestor. Then again, Carly wasn't sure the police would pay attention to her. Would the authorities view Adele as an elderly woman who grew afraid at every noise she heard in her old house?

Barely veiled panic colored Adele's voice. "Yes, yes, I'll do that."

Worry for her skittered through Carly. She'd promised Adele she'd be around if the woman had more trouble. "No, I'll call. And then I'll be right over. If he gets there before me, don't open the door," she instructed.

"I won't."

Carly dialed the police emergency number. With an assurance that officers would come, she slung Billy's diaper bag over her shoulder, tucked her evening purse under her arm and picked up Billy. Before closing the door behind her, she checked the clock on the kitchen wall. Time was paramount. She couldn't be late meeting Alex.

Chapter Fifteen

Where was she? Alex ambled away from the buzz of conversation in the living room of Bennett Doleman's home. Anxiety gripped him as his imagination breezed over all the dire possibilities that inevitably popped to mind when someone was late.

For the past half hour, terrifying images had intruded. With a moment alone, he stepped outside the living room's French doors and peered at his watch again. A knot tightened in the pit of his stomach more from worry than impatience. Where the hell was she?

"Here you are." The wind ruffled thin strands of Bennett Doleman's white hair. "Your wife did understand the importance of this evening, didn't she?" Doleman's thick eyebrows bunched with his frown. "Do you believe she might have forgotten?"

Alex wished that was what had happened.

"Webb and Mrs. Pipperton expected to see her here."

Alex shut out his words. He didn't want to hear criticism about her. He simply wanted to know she was safe. "If you'll excuse me, I would like to use your telephone," he answered in the calm, controlled tone that he'd mastered through the years.

"Of course. Use the one in the library." Doleman's hand suddenly closed over Alex's shoulder. "I must apologize. It's obvious you're worried, but she may be on her way."

Alex nodded agreeably because he didn't want to believe anything else.

Uneasiness shadowing him, he wound his way toward the library and the telephone. Every few steps, someone stopped him. He endured the handshakes, the pats on the back, but felt as if he were in a dark tunnel and to reach the light at the end of it, he had to get to that telephone.

His mood darkened before he freed himself from answering questions about where his wife was. He might have been embarrassed if he were not controlled by an emotion more intense—fear.

She'd had a flat tire. She'd gotten sidetracked. That seemed reasonable. She often dashed off to buy supplies or to take Billy to the park, then remembered an appointment.

Alex swore because none of that made sense. She'd bought a new dress. He'd called her to meet him. She wouldn't have forgotten. Something was wrong. With her? Or with Billy? God, the thought of something happening to either of them was too unbearable to consider.

Carly was perched on the arm of Adele's sofa and shot a look at the anniversary clock on the mantel. She was late. So were the police. Was Alex worrying? Or was he furious? Her heart quickened while she dug in her purse for the slip of paper with Bennett Doleman's address and phone number on it.

"Oh, my dear, I forgot." Adele's eyes looked bigger behind her thick lenses. "You're supposed to go to that dinner." She disappeared to check on Billy. Seconds ago, Carly had whisked into Adele's dining room and done the same thing to find him asleep in his carrier seat.

"You should leave," Adele called from the other room. "Tonight's important, isn't it?"

Carly appreciated Adele's concern, but she'd seen the fear in Adele's eyes. Until the police arrived, how could she leave? "It'll be all right," Carly said soothingly to keep the woman calm. Even if Vestor didn't come, the police would arrive. Adele couldn't handle this alone. "I need to use your telephone."

"Of course, but shouldn't you—" Reappearing in the doorway, Adele darted a look at the ringing phone.

While she answered it, Carly fished the sheet of paper from her purse and wandered to the window to peek outside. She saw no one, not even the police. What if she'd acted impulsively calling them? You never think of the consequences, her aunt had always said, as if that were a mortal sin. But how could she chance leaving without being sure Adele was safe? She had no way of knowing what Vestor would do. Would Alex understand? No, she didn't think so. He'd already warned her not to get involved.

"Carly?" Adele held the receiver out to her. "It's Alex."

Every anxious moment she'd had about this evening closed in on her.

"Carly?"

Hearing no anger in his tone, she relaxed. "Alex, I'm sorry that I'm late."

"Why are you still there? Has something happened?"

Nerves flip-flopped her stomach. "No, no, well—"

"Billy's all right?"

She heard the worry in his voice and ached that she'd caused it. "Yes, Alex, he's fine."

"Then why are you still there?" he repeated, sounding confused.

"I was dressed and ready to take Billy to Adele's when she called me. Vestor called her again."

"You didn't come because he made another phone call to her?" he asked incredulously.

She caught the change in his tone. "This was too important—"

"This was, too, for me."

Carly toyed with the telephone cord. "I didn't do this deliberately. I couldn't leave. I had no sitter for Billy." There was no way to avoid his anger. "Lisa is at the airport picking up her husband, and Adele couldn't take care of Billy."

"Because she was too upset?"

Reasonable. She sighed with relief that he sounded more reasonable. "Yes, she was. I called the police, but Adele needed someone." He was silent for so long, she thought he'd hung up and she'd missed the click. "Alex? She needed someone," she repeated, but he re-

...ained silent. "Could you explain to everyone that I ...ouldn't come?"

"How can I?" He released a sarcastic laugh. "When ...don't understand. I couldn't believe you wouldn't get ...ere if you could. Do you know what went through my ...ind? Do you know how worried I was that something ...ad happened to you?"

"I didn't mean to worry you. I was going to call ...ou."

"But you didn't."

The hurt in his voice swayed her as what he didn't say ...ame through clearly. *When I need you, you aren't here.* ...o caught up in her happiness with him, she'd barely ...onsidered the moment when he would rely on her to do ...he right thing and she would fail. Energy drained out ...f her. In his eyes, she'd made the supreme faux pas. ...he'd let him down. "Did they announce the new ...EO?"

"Me," he said with no pleasure.

Carly drew a hard breath. She wished she was there ...o hug him. "Should I come now?" she asked, sensing ...he hurt controlling him.

"Does it matter to you?"

Why couldn't he grasp that she'd had no choice, that ...he couldn't abandon someone who needed her? "I told ...ou." Carly spoke calmly. If she lost her temper, his ...ould flare more intensely. "He was threatening to ...ome."

"So you went there. Without knowing what you were ...alking into, you took my son there."

Carly sucked in a quick breath. *My son.* A pang of ...ain so intense it nearly buckled her, aroused anger. ...bruptly, she cut him off. "I did what I had to do.

And— Oh, God. Alex.'' Fear rushed up. "Alex, he's at her door. He's pounding on it and the police aren't here. Alex.'' She said his name, needing him so badly, she wanted to beg. At the click of the phone, she gripped the receiver tighter. "Alex,'' she said again, but expected no answer.

"Carly?'' Adele gasped at the hard pounding on her door. "What should we do?''

Carly wished she had Brian's baseball bat, anything. "I've called the police,'' she yelled out as she braved her way to the door.

"What will you do?'' Adele repeated on a sob. "The police aren't here and—''

Apprehension accompanied Carly's every step to the door. "Be calm,'' she said softly, amazing herself. Even as her heart thundered in her chest, she wrestled for courage. "I'll handle him.'' With a look over her shoulder, she urged Adele, "Take care of—'' Her words died on a whisper. Swiveling a look back at the door, she hardly had time to react as the chain snapped.

Hurling himself forward, Vestor banged into her and sent her sailing to her backside on the carpet.

Behind her, Adele screamed.

Carly scrambled to a stand and rushed to block his path to Adele. "Get out,'' she shouted, tipping her head back to meet Vestor's squinting look.

With a pockmarked face and slightly crooked nose that appeared to have been broken more than once, he towered over her. "Shut up!''

The size of him shredded Carly's bravado.

He shot a glare past her. "You, old lady,'' he said, pointing a meaty finger in Adele's direction, "you're the one I'm talkin' to. I'm tired of messin' around with you. My boss is comin' in and you're goin'—"

"Vestor, Vestor," another voice said from the doorway.

"Yessir." Vestor stepped back with one foot and gave Carly a brief view of a shorter balding man.

"You must remain calm." Dressed in an expensive suit, the man appeared docile and nonthreatening, but his voice held an edge of malice. "It's time for a serious talk. It's Mrs. Bridelman, isn't it?"

Her back to a corner wall, Adele nodded.

"I will make you a generous offer that you won't be able to resist."

"And what if she does?" Carly demanded to know, craning her neck to see around Vestor's bulky frame.

The man glared at Vestor. "I thought you said she lives alone."

"She does, boss."

"Then *who* is this?"

Carly tipped up her chin. "I'm a friend and neighbor."

He slitted his eyes. "A nosy one."

Carly prodded herself to step closer. "She doesn't want to sell."

His lips curved at the corners. "Minding your own business might be healthier for—" The wail of a siren silenced him. Whipping around, he stared at the door. As the siren grew louder, he whirled back to Carly. "You called the police?"

Looking confused, Vestor did a nervous dance in place. "She said she did, Mr. Dorn."

"Fool!" Dorn swore at Vestor and scurried toward the door. "We'll finish this business later." He opened

the door and stood face-to-face with two men in blue.
Carly nearly flew at them in gratitude.

Blocking Vestor's and Dorn's escape, a policeman
who looked almost a decade younger than her, asked,
"Trouble, ma'am?"

Tension pouring out of her, she let her shoulders relax. "Plenty," she answered in a voice weaker than
usual.

Alex sprinted from his car. During the phone call, he
couldn't help the feeling building inside him or give her
the understanding she wanted. He hadn't been thinking about the people at the party or how they would
view her absence. He'd been dealing with an ache he'd
known in his youth and had thought he would never feel
again. Now, the only emotion gripping him was fear.

Trailing one step behind two men in suits, he brushed
past them, ignoring their glares, and charged into the
house. Relief swamped him. Holding Billy, Carly was
leaning against a wall. Though pale, she didn't look so
much hurt as manhandled.

"Who are you?" one of the suits asked him while
flashing his detective's identification at Alex.

"Her husband," he answered, breaking the combative stare with him to meet Carly's eyes. "Are you all
right?"

Carly's heart lurched. Though his eyes floated over
her as if reassuring himself she was telling the truth, she
saw no warmth. An ache spiraled through her. She'd
had a reprieve from the stunning despair she'd felt during their phone call. Now her mind rushed back to his
angry words. "I'm fine." But she wasn't, and it had
nothing to do with Vestor or the other man. Was it

possible for the heart to break? She'd always thought that was simply an expression, yet overwhelming sorrow crowded her.

"So what happened then?" one of the detectives asked Carly, insisting on her attention.

"He burst through the door." Her voice trembling, she gripped the edge of Adele's mantel to keep her legs from buckling beneath her.

The detective's eyes darted to Adele. "That's when he threatened you?"

"Threatened both of us. They're both contemptible, vile men," Adele said with a newfound indignation.

Stony-faced, the detective barely veiled his amusement. "Yes, ma'am. They were a pair. We've had a few complaints against them."

"Then why weren't they in jail?" Adele snapped.

"No one was willing to press charges, and upset older folks usually can't give us a detailed enough accounting to prove anything."

Adele glared in response. "We're not all senile, young man." Her back ramrod straight, she let her irritation slide out. "Tell me why he wants my property."

"Dorn's been buying oceanfront property cheap to build condominiums. You can guess how. Intimidation made him successful. Vestor prided himself on frightening owners to accept his boss's offers."

The detective's gaze shifted to Carly. "Are you willing to testify, too?"

The idea knotted Carly's stomach, but she answered the only way that she could. "Of course I will."

"Good. Then we can finally bring a case against Dorn and Vestor."

Nerves frayed, Carly skirted a policeman. They had her name and address. There was no reason for her to stay. As Billy whimpered in her arms, she picked up his carrier seat from the dining room floor. She needed time to herself, time to think.

At the clatter of the back screen door closing, Alex sidestepped a cop blocking his path to the dining room.

"Hey, where you going?"

"I'll be back," Alex snapped. With a few quick steps, he passed through the room and checked the kitchen. Not finding Carly, he wanted to run out the door. He made himself go back through the living room.

Police again blocked his way as they filed out of Adele's house. Though impatience surged through Alex, he resisted barging his way past them.

"Alex." Adele snagged his arm. "Could I speak with you for a minute?"

Suddenly, even one minute seemed too long.

As if matching Carly's mood, rain came down in huge drops before she reached the house. Tired, she settled Billy in the playpen in the kitchen and heated herself a cup of coffee. She tried to understand everything Alex was feeling. She'd expected his disappointment with her. After all, she'd let him down. To his way of thinking, she'd acted impulsively. And what she'd feared most had happened. When she hadn't done as expected, someone she cared about had turned away from her.

What would he want now? Would he want her to leave? *My son.* Over and over, she kept hearing those words in her head. An ache swelled inside her. This child is mine, too, she'd wanted to shout back at him, for in her heart Billy was hers. With a finger, she stroked Billy's hand and thought about all she wanted, all that seemed to be slipping from her grasp again.

"I'm so grateful to Carly," Adele said for what seemed like the umpteenth time. "What would I have done without her?"

What would he do without her? Alex wondered, unable to forget the hurt he'd seen in her eyes before she'd whisked out of Adele's home.

"Carly didn't say too much, but I assumed you were angry at her. Please don't be."

Lightly Alex squeezed the elderly woman's arm to soothe her anxiousness. "I'm not angry."

"I must have misunderstood then. I thought—" She waved a hand in an offhand manner. "I'm glad. I wouldn't want to be responsible for causing any trouble between you two. You're such a nice family."

"Are you going to be okay?" he asked as he inched his way to the door.

"Oh, I'm fine. Go, go," she urged, even gently nudging his arm.

Alex charged out the door but took only a few steps as Lisa Robets rushed up to him. A wide-eyed Brian and a concerned-looking man who Alex assumed was Gordon lagged behind her.

"Alex, we saw the police cruisers. What's happened?" Lisa asked excitedly.

"Adele could use some company."

Lisa grabbed the sleeve of Alex's tuxedo. "Is she all right?"

"She's fine now."

"Vestor was here?"

Alex shot an anxious look at his house. He didn't want to explain. The need to see Carly seeped into every part of his being. "Adele will tell you everything."

Lisa's gaze followed his. "And Carly's okay?"

"Why wouldn't she be?"

"I assumed she was here with Adele. Carly promised her that she would be here if she was needed."

"Yes, she was here." That was Carly. It was that simple to describe her. If someone needed her, she would be there. "She's at home. She's okay, too."

Walking toward the house, he swore softly. Since the phone call, he'd wished more times than he could count for his words back. Why had he overreacted? Why had he been so judgmental about her behavior with Billy? Nothing had happened to the child.

He walked slower, letting the rain pour over him as blame pressed down heavily on him. Pride, not anger, had made him act like a fool and yell those words at her. That she'd placed someone else's needs above his had hurt.

He'd been insensitive. Dumb. He could think of a dozen more things to call himself for lashing out with words that would tear at her and for saying the one thing that would cut her the deepest. *My son,* he'd said. Mine.

Sure Billy was his, but hadn't she given up everything to stay with the child, to prove how much she loved him? She'd always been there for Billy. And in typical Carly fashion, she'd weighed the moment this evening and had been there for the person who'd needed her most.

He hadn't been fair to her. She'd done the best she could. But then, the words he'd said hadn't really been meant for her. Never her, he realized in a flash of insight, but for his mother who'd never been there for him.

Nearing the house, he acknowledged one agonizing fact. She hadn't let him down; he'd let her down.

The click of the back door roused Carly from a chair in the kitchen. She didn't want to look into his eyes. Mostly she didn't want more angry words to pass between them. She glanced at Billy in his playpen, then snatched up a dish towel to busy herself with the dishes in the drain rack.

Alex wiped a hand across his damp face. Seconds ticked by as silence hung between them. He watched her brush her cheek with the back of her hand. Because he'd been more prepared for her anger, guilt that he'd caused the tears gripped him. "Carly."

"The evening didn't go exactly as planned." And he did prefer things to go according to plan, she reminded herself. With her, he would never know what to expect. Was he realizing that?

"Want to start over?" he asked to calm the mood.

"It won't change anything." Carly tightened her hold on the dish towel. Dreams she'd allowed herself to believe in had slipped away in a few short hours as uncomfortably he'd revived all the criticism aimed at her as a child. "I learned something about myself tonight." Her words came out strangled. "You needed me to be the type of person I'd rebelled against being through my whole childhood." She fought a twinge of weakness that made her want to rush into his arms. "But I can't change for you, Alex. I want to. I want to be the kind of woman you need in your life, but I can't give you what you need."

Alex took a step closer. She'd only given him laughter and love. She'd changed him, brought fun into his life, taught him to laugh at himself, to reach out to his son. "Did I ever ask you to change?" Anger at himself rose within him. "I thought we'd begun to share enough that we could get through bad moments. Was I wrong?"

"No, you aren't. But your career means so much to you." Carly labored for a breath. "I'm sorry. Like tonight, I could jeopardize—"

The apology pricked him. "Don't."

Her heart stopped, but because dodging anything wasn't her style, she faced him. "I really am."

In a gesture so familiar, he ached watching it, she tucked strands of her hair behind her ear. "I don't want your apology," he said, wishing for the warmth he usually saw in her face.

Confusion made her step back and reach for the kitchen counter.

"Isn't marriage dealing with good and bad moments, sticking it out?" he asked.

An ache pierced her, not for herself, but for him as she realized he was thinking about his parents.

For a long moment, Alex stared into her eyes. "You told me you loved me. Do you still?"

She shook her head. "Love isn't something a person switches on and off."

"At one time, I thought it was." At one time, he'd believed differently. He'd thought nothing lasted forever.

Serious eyes, she mused. "Because of your parents?"

"It's a good excuse." Discomfort tightened like a hard ball in the center of his stomach. Defenses built through the years shattered. She'd inched her way into his life, and now he couldn't imagine a day, an hour, a minute without her. "I was wrong, not you." How could he explain? Once he'd heard her voice, his anxiousness over her safety had mingled with fury over her foolishness. He hadn't had a callous disregard for Adele. He'd been worried about his wife. Hell, he'd been frantic.

Desperately, Carly wanted him to understand. "I couldn't leave her."

"I know. I really do," he said softly.

"You do? You didn't think it was irresponsible and—"

He cut her off. "Caring. Loving. Special." He captured her eyes with his steadfast stare. "I think you're the most special person in the world." He moved to the counter to stand inches from her. On a long breath, he brushed a knuckle across her cheek. "Carly, I'm trying to tell you." He grappled with patience. "Because you love me, I know you wouldn't hurt me intentionally. And because I love you, I don't want you to change. It's because of you that I have everything I could want. Because of you, I learned what loving my son really means."

Breathing suddenly seemed difficult as she craved to feel his arms around her.

"You gave more than I expected, more than I'd ever had in my life. More than I deserve." To have her, to have all he'd found because of her, he spoke his every thought. "How can I find fault with you when who you

are, the way you give so much to other people, is one of
the reasons I fell in love with you?''

Carly saw in the darkness of his eyes the truth in his
words, the warmth of love. Here was the giving, the
unconditional love she'd always longed for.

The sight of her smile encouraged Alex. Until that
second, he hadn't realized how much he'd needed the
softness of her lips beneath his.

Long and thorough, the kiss bound them in a way no
marriage license or night of passion ever would. As
emotion linked them, joy swelled inside her. He loved
her despite what had happened. That message was in
the gentleness of his kiss, in the desperation of his arms
around her.

''Believe me,'' he whispered against her mouth. ''I
love you just the way you are.''

Tilting her head back, Carly laughed. ''You're very
convincing,'' she said softly, tracing his smile.

A clatter behind them jerked their attention toward
the door.

Head bent, Dora shuffled in, banging her suitcase
against the doorjamb. ''I'm back,'' she announced
merrily. ''Did anything exciting happen while I was
gone...?'' Her voice trailed off, her smile deepening at
the sight of them still in each other's arms. ''Guess
that's a dumb question. Looks to me like plenty of excitement happened while I was gone.''

Billy babbled gleefully from his playpen.

''Oh, I missed you.'' Dora bent over and lifted him
into her arms. ''Did you miss me?''

Grinning, he gurgled.

''Phew,'' she said, wrinkling her nose. ''Some things
haven't changed. You're still the sweetest-looking little

boy. But smelly," she added with a glance at Alex and Carly. "I'll change him."

Alex laughed as she ambled out with Billy in her arms. "Our son has perfect timing," he said.

Our son. Carly pressed her cheek to his again and savored those words. "Why does he have perfect timing?"

Inhaling her scent as if he would never get enough of it, Alex buried his face in her hair. "Because he knew I wanted to do this." Again, he kissed her. Quick and hard and filled with a different kind of urgency. "Now, come with me," he said, taking her hands in his and drawing her toward the back door.

She sniffed with feigned disdain. "We're going to walk in the rain again?"

Alex's eyes narrowed. "Close your eyes."

"Close my—" Smiling, Carly did as she was told. "I love surprises."

His hand at her waist, he walked her outside. "I guessed that."

She felt a drop of rain hit her face but knew they hadn't walked far. She'd been counting her steps.

"Okay, open your eyes."

Still standing with her beneath the overhang, he touched her shoulders and aimed her toward the shadowed end of the driveway, toward what he'd had delivered while he was at the party.

Carly's heart skipped at the sight of the huge electric kiln. "Alex—"

Laughing, he squeezed her shoulder. "Is it all right?"

She didn't answer. She ran into the downpour to reach the kiln, and inspected it with a child's wonderment. She'd struggled so long without it, always having to find a cooperative artist to fire her work. Now she had her own kiln. But it was more than the kiln smarting tears in her eyes. While it represented his belief in her work, it meant so much more to her. Here was another token of his gift for giving, his acceptance of who she was.

Standing near, Alex watched her run a smoothing hand over the equipment in the same tender way she stroked Billy's head. "Now you have everything you need."

Carly turned into Alex's arms. "Yes, I have everything." She touched his face. "I have you and Billy."

Pleased, Alex tugged her against him. "Thank you," he murmured, sliding his hands down her arms.

"What for?" Carly asked brightly.

"For loving me even when I was an idiot."

"For better or for worse," she said on a soft sigh. That vow suddenly held a deeper meaning for her. He loved her. Nothing that happened would take that love away.

Alex lowered his head. "For a lifetime," he murmured and sought her mouth again.

*   *   *   *   *